# IN DREAMS WE SLEEP

*Dominc Lyne*

# In Dreams
# We Sleep

||||||||||||||||||||||||||||||||||||||||||||||||||||||||||||||||||||||||||||||||||||||||||||||||||||||||

New Orleans

Published in the United States of America by
Queer Space
A Rebel Satori Imprint
www.rebelsatoripress.com

This is a work of fiction. Names, characters, places, and incidents are the product of the author's imagination and are used fictitiously and any resemblance to actual persons, living or dead, business establishments, events, or locales is entirely coincidental. The publisher does not have any control over and does not assume any responsibility for author or third-party websites or their content.

Cover image by Isidoro Martínez.

Library of Congress Control Number: 2020944482

# CHAPTER ONE

*Eyes open, awake. Shit. Focus. Where am I? Check, tap down all important areas. Keys, wallet, phone. Cock, ass. None have been taken, none have been used. Sit back, relax. Breathe. Focus.*

*Shit, fuck, hell. Where am I? Calm. No point panicking, everything is good. How can it be good? I have no clue where I am. Calm. Calm. Breathe. It'll all come back when it's ready. You are not hurt therefore there is no danger.*

*Pull out a packet of cigarettes. Open. Take one, place it between lips. Lighter. Click, flame, inhale. Hold. Count to five. One, two, three, four, five. Exhale. Feels good. Euphoria. Lungs bleeding and all the mind can do is take pleasure. Another drag, then another. Starting to feel normal again. Good. Smoke to the butt then flick away, its corpse explodes in a sea of orange sparks.*

*So think. Click that brain into gear and see what it can do for this situation. Nothing. Okay, location. Street, no, alleyway. Squashed between a bin and air-con unit. Good choice. Weather. Raining, can see it hitting the street in front. Quite heavy. Good choice to hide in shelter. Hide? No, not hide, that doesn't feel right. Brain working. Click, click, whirr.*

Flashback.

*Scoring. Syringe in hand; connect to needle. Smile. Check location, alone. Night. Good. Needle through skin, push. Deep sigh. Done.*

Present.

*Ah crap. Look at arm. Pokka-dotted with tiny pinpricks. One looks like it is going to track. Shit. Must watch out for that, don't want a major infection on our hands. So yeah, recent history solved. That's all that matters for now.*

*Work another cigarette into the mouth. Click, flame, inhale. Exhale. Smoke this then make a move. It is late, or is that early? Either way it's time to get on. Do not know how long I have been crashed out here. Food. Oh yeah, food would be so good right now. Food, piss and a big fat crap. What more could you ask for? Well, besides sex, what more could you ask for?*

*Shit, fuck. Where am I? Oh yeah. Alleyway. Right, move. Pushing up off the ground and standing up. Stagger, move forward. Gain control of the feet before we hit reality. Fuck, that must have been some good shit. Smile.*

Niente sits on the Tube train, the last carriage always less crowded, everyone groups together around the middle like herded cattle staying together for safety. That is the way he likes it, especially given the state of him. He cannot look his best after sitting in the alleyway, his jeans splattered with street dirt, the needle marks visible on his arm. He notes he has lost his jacket. *Fuck it,* he thinks. *Do I really give a shit?*

The train glides smoothly across its tracks, quietly moving along to the hum of electricity. He smiles, mankind having to travel like rats through a sewer because their above ground world is too densely populated. In all honesty he can never understand why so many still get in their cars and sit in traffic when it is so much easier, and cheaper, to travel underground. *Old habits die hard,* he guesses.

He looks up; people are staring at him, their faces filled with disdain. After all this time people are still disgusted by those who stand out, the individual still forced to conform, to fit in. So much easier to be like everyone else, to think like everyone else than to actually act as you want, to actually embrace the freedoms you used to have. All around him businessmen, power suited women, slaves to a wage. Money the god of mankind, greed its morals. So much stress and worry in their lives, so much anger. Where did the fun go? Left at the wayside as they got absorbed into the mechanics of the system. Soul prisons waiting for the day they die, ashamed to embrace their true nature, filled with regrets about the dreams they lost, the self created burdens on their shoulders slowly corroding their will. Mice running scared from the dark, the unknown, creating reasons for their existence. If only they knew how pitiful they looked. *Lost souls now govern the Earth.*

He looks down the carriage, ignores the two headed creature crouched at the end eating the brains of some woman with pure gluttony. It pauses, eyeballs him. *It doesn't exist,* he thinks, *it can't.* Eyes back to the carriage, the real carriage. *All these fuckers just live in their own private worlds without care for anyone but themselves, their needs greater than anything.* Niente could drop dead in front of them, get shot or attacked and no one would lift a finger to help, they would just move away from the scene as quickly as they could and pretend it had never happened. They would even have the nerve to complain bitterly when people did it to them. Parasites, taking all they need and leaving nothing in return. Lice building their communities and bleeding their host dry, sucking away, causing nothing but pain and discomfort. *How did it ever get to this stage?*

The train stops, people rise and exit, continuing on with their lives, the time spent and faces seen underground an insignificant moment to their day. People leave, more arrive, life replacing life constantly. So many names, lives, so many strangers. Niente stares into the darkness outside the window as the train pulls away from the station. So much darkness. He sits locked in his own thoughts and solitude. You never feel more alone than when you are surrounded by swarms of people. He sighs and holds onto the pole by his seat. The train slows; he gets to his feet. This is his stop. Doors open, he makes his forgettable exit.

Back home Niente crumbles onto the sofa and sighs. He rolls his eyes to the digital clock hanging from the wall. 8am, it took him longer to get home than he had expected, no, not expected, hoped. He scratches his arm, lets his eyes fall down. Bugs, creatures crawling on him, poking their ant-like heads out of the vicious marks and pulling themselves free before scuttling away. He stops scratching. No point attacking something that is not really there.

*Fuck, shit.* Maybe he should sleep. He feels tired. *Bed, yes, bed is good.* He stands, he walks, he sees. *What the fuck?* A tear, a dark split across the room. A hole in a canvas. He can feel his face crawl into a frown. *Hallucination.* That seems the logical explanation. He turns his back on it. If it is still there in the morning he will deal with it then.

His eyes heavy, he is asleep before he even hits the bed.

*Dream.*
Wake. Eyes open. Factory, no, not factory, there is a bar

lined with shadows. Figures of mist ordering drinks in a language he does not know. *Great. Perfect, just what I need. No, exactly what I need, a bar and no one to disturb me. Awesome.*

Drink. Double vodka, lemon mixer. The idea is not to get drunk too quickly. Sip, look around. Light, bright light. Cool bar, so much space that it all feels swamped.

'Can you not feel it?'

*Great, that's all I fucking need.* He slowly looks around him, trying to find to find the source of the voice. A woman, old, sits next to him, a smouldering cigarette gripped tightly between two fingers of her right hand, her face lined with wrinkles, deep set like trenches on a war field. 'Pardon?' Niente croaks.

'Can you not feel it?'

'Don't get you, sorry.'

'You have brought it here. Brought it with you and that is perfect.'

'What the hell are you on about?' Niente looks around searching for the 'it' he is meant to have brought with him. He cannot see it so he looks back. The stool next to him is empty. *What the fuck?*

'Can you not see it?'

Niente's head spins around, the woman is sat on the opposite side, different clothes, black instead of white, her wrinkles deeper, face more emaciated. A skin covered skull. She puts her fingers to her lips to silence any comeback. 'You will see eventually. You will understand.'

'Understand what exactly?'

She pats him on the shoulder with a bony hand as she stands and walks away. Walking into the shadows that creep in from the corners, edging slowly towards him. He turns his back on her.

His glass empty, he orders a refill. Knocks it back and demands another.

*Reality.*

Television screen flickers. Static burst. Digital snowstorm. Volume on mute. Silence. Dead silence. A hand holds a remote. No movement. Cold, hollow, brittle. No thoughts, no desire to change the channel. Snowflake follows snowflake.

Outside the road lays silent. The only light the blue flickers coming from the houses. A ghost town. A pitiful light in an ocean of darkness. Timeless. Dead. Silent. Figures move. Shadows within shadows. Whispers. Quiet whispers like wind. Then nothing.

The blue dies and everything fades to black.

Niente awakes. His eyes open with a snap. Movement. He hears movement. He sits up sharply. A shadow darts across the wall. He is out of bed in an instant. The digital display of his bedside clock tells him it is 8pm. *Fuck, another day lost to sleep.* His legs feel weak. It is that time again. *No, I'll resist. I'll be good.* From a drawer he pulls out a blue pill and swallows dry. *That'll take the edge off.*

*Right, where was I? The shadow.* He moves through the dark flat slowly. He notices the blue flickering from the living room. At the door he sees it. The television tuned to a dead channel, filling the space with its dull light.

It is still there. The tear. Bigger, running the whole length of the room. A noise grows around him. A dirty noise, warped and beating like a twisted heartbeat. He grabs at his remote. Finger on button the television refuses to shut down. The volume refuses to lower, getting louder instead.

*Fucking thing.* He takes a step towards it. Hesitates. He will have to walk past the tear to get to it. *Shit.* He wipes his hand down his face. *Fuck it; it's only a hallucination. What the fuck am I scared of?*

With new determination he marches towards the flickering box. He was wrong; he never reaches it.

# CHAPTER TWO

*There.*

The woman with three eyes is staring at him. *Fucking bitch.* She rubs her breasts together as she hangs in a seated position from the ceiling suspended by meat hooks.

'You will not find your answers here.' That voice again. That wizened old hag. Niente tells her to fuck off without turning his attention away from the hanging creature.

With a scream the woman's skin peels off and she falls to the ground, her skin hanging like a fur coat after the raping of its soul. The bloody body stands and grabs at its newly revealed cock. Tugging sharply on its erection before pointing to a member of the audience, beckoning with a salacious curl of its finger. The chosen man moves forward and bends to suck, taking the cock into his mouth. He gags for a moment then his body goes limp, corroding as it falls dead against the floor, its skin rotting. Cum leaks out of the decaying O. The crowd cheers. The performer bows gracefully. Embracing the calls for an encore it pulls the volunteer's trousers off and looks at the shrivelled flesh. Its cock goes hard. It fucks it until only dust is left. The audience cheers with rapture.

Niente stands there with his mouth open. *What the fuck just happened?* The stage lights dim as the next act is prepared for. He turns away from the stage. That hag is still there, propping up the bar, a cigarette hanging from her lips. She looks younger this time. She gestures to the glass next to her; he takes up her offer of a drink.

'Still here then?' he says.

'Why would I not be?' She exhales a trail of blue smoke. 'Did you find the answer?'

'I'm not looking for answers.'

'Oh, you will.' She giggles a hoarse laugh.

'What?' Niente grabs her arm and turns her towards him sharply. Her neck snaps on its brittle spine and hangs limp on her shoulders.

'How do you expect me to finish my cigarette now you asshole?' she spits as the half smoked cancer stick hits the ground.

He lets go of her and she falls against the bar, another snap in her spine and she ends up in a heap on the floor. *Oops* is all he can think. *Now what?* How is he meant to know what she was going on about? *Shit.*

A hand grabs his shoulder. It belongs to a bouncer. He lifts him off his feet. 'Right buddy, I think you've had enough to drink.' Dragged through the room, he gets thrown out the bar into an alleyway. A boot in his back to make the fact even more clear. Niente crawls a few paces and pull himself up with the aid of a gravestone.

*What?* He spins around, the club and alleyway gone. Stood in the centre of a graveyard. *What?*

Pain. A sharp pain cutting through. *Shit, the pill's wearing off.* He just needs a hit. One hit and then he will try and make sense of all this. 'Try' being the operative word in this case. Another jab of pain. *Shit.*

His eyes look down at his arms as they hang limp like dead snakes. *What the fuck is going on here?* The left snake curls and wraps around the right, easing its itching, its craving. He falls to the ground in pain. 'Oh fuck,' he whimpers.

*Look at me, collapsed here, head in my hands, rivers falling down skin.* Alone, sobering. The dead around him may like to listen but never will their bodies reply. Deep in his head the demons set up camp, inescapable. His hand claws down his face. *So, I was meant to find answers was I? Well give me the answer to this you fuckers.* 'What is happening?' he screams into the void.

The silence is unbearable; its air thick with the anticipation of reply but nothing comes. No warm stream of blood pours from its wounds, his words just holes slashed through a canvas. The silence, such silence. Planet on mute, judgment postponed until further notice. What had he been expecting? A fanfare of commotion as God finally gets off his ass and tumbles chaotically to the ground? Maybe he is too late; maybe he asked the wrong question.

'Why?' he screams, his voice hoarse. 'Why is all this shit happening?'

One final plea and then salvation.

He lets his eyes close, no dreams come, a world of black shadows. Figures moving, peering in to look at his face before melting back into the darkness. Whispers, voices, a language unknown to his brain, ebbing and flowing into his ears; a hum of noise, thick, dirty. The darkness melts away and he finds himself sat in the middle of a road. Houses stretch into the distance along both sides. Tall shadowy buildings sheltering life from the elements. The flicker of television screens the only light, a dull blue, weak, pitiful.

Something tells him that the lives that existed inside those houses is past tense. When it had existed it had been standard life. The tainted 9 to 5 life filled with the simple series of tasks completed each day. Life in monotony. Wake up, work, TV, sleep. Everything structured around days – payday, rent day, Friday piss ups. How did it ever end up like that? Sometimes he used to wish he could connect with that world, jump on its conveyor belt and be a 'respected' member of society. To join the clones in their brain-dead quest to achieve nothing but a feeling of self worth. He guesses that at this moment that is a wish he wants more than any desire. *What the fuck am I thinking? To be absorbed into the system and live without dreams, without hope, without direction? Sod that.* He is not designed to conform, he is not programmed to just sit back and follow orders.

He sits in the still silence watching the houses. *Why am I being shown this? What is trying to be proved?* He repeats his earlier question. 'Why? Why is this shit happening? Why am I here to see it?'

As he speaks, the world flickers. Static burst. His vision blurs and refocuses. Sat in a solid but plush armchair, his arms chained to its arms. Before him a single building. Large, surrounded by darkness. The front of the building crumbles to dust revealing the interior, a cross section of life in a block of flats, each room filled with life. People going about their business unaware. Rats in their cages watched like television.

From the darkness that noise. Low, growing in volume. That twisted sound, dirty, throbbing. A dull pulse. The heartbeat of the shadows. The first scream cuts into the air. The woman had been so harmless, stepping naked into the shower and turning on the tap. The gas melted her to nothing. It made the cuts on her wrist seem so pointless.

Scream follows scream. His eyes pan across the scene.

Families sat in front of dead television sets, masks pumping green gas into their lungs through tubes running like cables through the flats. Mother places the plate in front of her smiling daughter whilst Father attaches the mask to her face; in his bedroom their son hangs from the ceiling, the severed tube round his neck whilst its other half fills the room with its exhaust fumes.

Then he sees it, a face, someone he knows. A face from his past. A face he loved. Dark skinned and sitting in a room alone, head in his hands, the tears pouring between his fingers. His head raises, tears of blood falling from rotten eyes, mouth stitched shut with a shoelace. A solitary cross of thickly woven thread keeping his lips together. He leans back on the bed and grabs at his erect cock. Jacking off as his skin peels like paint curling off a wall.

Niente screams as he tries to rip free from the armchair. Screaming to be able to save that one life. Screaming, his eyes forced to look. Forced to see the skin curl and peel from the bones that crumble to dust after his final empty ejaculation. The force at which they crumble causes clouds of their ash to erupt into the sky, rising high on an invisible wind.

A voice. That voice. *Her* voice. 'So now you want answers? All that you see, they live in the darkness. Exist in nothing. Their souls dead, minds like dream cemeteries, their final moments on constant repeat. All their hopes lost in rotten caskets locked in the past. Creatures with no direction endlessly seeking meaning. Some of us are marked; we are the Chosen. Key players destined to make change. That is why. There is your answer. You are different in more ways than you imagine.'

'Chosen?' Niente replies, his eyes scanning for the source

of the voice. 'Are you saying all those lives were meaningless?'

The voice continues. 'Each night as they laid on their backs praying silent prayers of forgiveness to gods they didn't even know whether or not they believed in, they failed to comprehend that one day it would end. That their wasted words fall into dear ears.'

'Dead ears?'

'Your gods sit on their thrones, limp arms hanging by their sides, guns locked in atrophied hands, the self created bullet wounds long since dried up. And what did you all expect? A god of peace and love to just sit and watch his angst-ridden children destroy his creation? At first he had turned his back, but then you placed the pistol in his hand and coaxed him to use its solitary bullet. Two bombs dropped, drops of black rain fell from the heavens, the blood from divine abandon.

'Lost souls then governed this world and their hearts were blackened with greed. The Earth is no longer young. It is old and dying, a billion year existence destroyed by two thousand years of human advancement. But its evil existed long before man, long before the wise serpent. The evil was there, lurking in the corners, hidden by the shadows. Mankind grew stupid, arrogant. Blackened to its core the darkness grew and called the eternal. Destruction bred destruction and the darkness claimed what was its own.'

Niente is confused, lost. A voice from nowhere putting all these images in his head. 'I don't understand. How does all that relate to me? Dead gods and lost souls?'

'The world now turns in silence. I never said the gods were dead. All his anger-filled children were abandoned; they stood alone without help against the darkness from which they were born. Nothing exists out there. Nothing.'

He laughs. 'Don't give me the whole "everything is in your head and you're the only one" bullshit.'

'No, you are not alone but you will see. You need to. Then you must make them see, make them understand. The lost need a shepherd to follow. Your piece is ready to be played.

'Be warned creatures of deceit.' The voice increases in its loudness, preaching to the flock of nothing, the block of flats long since demolished to the ground. 'Be warned of two brothers born of flesh and bone. Shattered halos on ebony snow. Red blood from which a devil's head will rise. Remember incidents that tore morals apart and pray for silence in their wake.

'One stands alone, abandoned he observes. Mind like tree roots locked in misanthropy. Words of truth through mouth of perfect face.

'The second flies high, winged death casting its shadow across the land through tormented eyes.

'Pray death for the time has come.'

Silence follows. Niente sits in the darkness, one tear falling from his eye whilst all around him ash falls like snow.

Eyes snap open, light blinding. A blinding white fading, focusing. Sat on the floor. Usual. Tap down. Nothing missing, nothing used. Slightly pre-cummy but ignore that. Awake? Home? Focus, concentrate. So he is sat on the ground, the solid base damp, cold. The caress of consecrated earth; a soil born from rot and decay. All around him stone slabs rise crookedly from the ground, the teeth of mortality, damaged, unkempt. New life growing upon carved obituaries. Place one foot on the Earth and it will devour you, slowly pull you down into the dirt.

*Shit, still here. Fuck, what?*

He wipes his eye and feels the frozen tear, a solitary crystalline memory. Without seeing a reflection he knows his eyes will be bloodshot, his face lined with the dried marks of despair. They say the dead always listen, feeling the world turn from within they cry their silent tears. Discarded husks abandoned in walled cemeteries. Safe under the watchful gaze of their god but locked in the past, memories that fade with each passing day. Only the dead have no future to call their own. For some reason that feels kind of symbolic.

He pulls himself to his feet. *This is totally fucked up. Totally.* The smell of cigarette smoke hits his nose. Instantly he reaches for his pockets but a pat of all of them proves that he has no pack to call his own. He searches for the source of the smell. His heart sinks when he sees it. *Her.* Sat on a gravestone, cigarette in one hand, vodka in the other. She smiles smugly at him as he walks towards her.

'I take it you want a cigarette?' she asks. Her face flatter, younger, now in her forties. She smiles again as she hands him a cigarette, the corners of her eyes crinkling up.

He takes it. Click, flame, inhale. Hold. Exhale. 'So, what was, *is,* all this about?'

She swigs on her drink but says nothing.

'I'm hallucinating right? In some drug dream. This can't be happening. What is this?'

'It is whatever you want it to be, as long as you get it.'

'That's it, *I don't.*'

'You will.'

'Speak sense.'

'Why? To make it all easy for you?'

Inhale. Hold. Exhale. 'Great. What are you, my guardian

angel? Some weird spirit guide designed to make me stop taking drugs? Great, of everything I could imagine, I conjure up you.'

'I am neither. Why would I want you stop? You need to keep using to actually see. It will break down more of the barriers.' She hops off the gravestone and takes one look at her empty glass. 'Well, I think I am done here. I need to find a refill.' She begins to walk away. She stops and turns back. 'Find the answers to these questions and you will get it. When was the last time there was something decent on television? And, when was the last time you left the city?'

# CHAPTER THREE

*Reality.*

Niente wakes with a start. His groggy eyes focus on the clock on his bedside table. 5:15 am. With a groan he turns over, pulling his blanket tighter around him. There is no way he is getting up. His mind pauses. How did he end up back in bed?

In his head he runs over what he had seen. The face rotting before him, the building crumbling to dust. *What could it all mean?* Had he really woken up? Had the television actually been on? Did he just dream it all? He sighs. Too much to think about. He reaches into a drawer. One pill missing, he frowns as he swallows another. It will tide him over until later. He definitely feels different, like he has something he needs to do, a meaning to his existence. The feeling washes over him and he tries to feel an emotion.

So, what is he supposed to do? Is he just to accept the burden of *her* words at the age of twenty-eight? Niente rises from the bed; there does not seem much point in lying there now he is wide awake. Forced sleep would only make the visions worse. He looks at the clock. 6 am. How quickly time flies when you have so much on your mind.

The day is still dark; the world's slow turn welcoming the city to the first kisses of daylight. Niente scratches his back as he stands naked before the window. His eyes scanning the faces of buildings, their empty eyes look vacantly back in his direction. Buildings have seen the lives of many. Hollow cases of memories, private life burnt into their internal fabric, public life passing them daily.

He pushes open the window, the fresh morning air rushing in, caressing his flesh. He feels his skin tighten at its touch. He listens to the sound of the moving traffic. People on their way to work, the early starts in an attempt to avoid the rush hour. He smiles, how disappointed they all would have been, all those writers imagining hovering cars and roads in the sky, buildings of pure glass rising like glaciers towards the heavens. It has been almost four hundred years since man had built the first factory and here they all are, still building with bricks and mortar, still driving around in wheeled cars on over congested roads, still building factory towers pumping toxic fumes into the atmosphere. Forty decades since the Industrial Revolution and mankind has not learnt.

Niente turns away from the window and walks back over to his bed. He sits down. Some writers had been right about one thing, the loss of freedom, lives caught on camera the moment you step outside, not even feeling in control of your own life. He tries to think about what life would be like had the eyes of the Council not been everywhere, what it would be like to live in freedom, even if it was a hollow notion, a beautiful lie.

Niente remembers reading about the first two great wars, wars that involved every nation on the planet. Wars fighting to protect their liberties, their freedoms, to halt the era of the dictators. After all the lives lost fighting, mankind still let those values slip away. Everything lost they just carried on their lives without care. He realizes he has never voted in an election. He cannot even picture the faces that make up the Council that govern the nation with their iron grip.

The Council has always been in power during the almost three decades of his life and without opposition they would obviously continue to remain that way. Ten people governing a nation without contest, could you imagine how they feel? All that power at their disposal. And yet, they have remained quiet for three years.

He glances back at his clock's digital display. Groaning he falls back on the bed. 6:30am. He reaches for his phone and dials in One's number. As it rings, he realizes he is still naked.

'Have you any idea of the time, Niente?' One mutters sleepily into the phone. He casts his eyes back to his clock and groans.

'I can't sleep, I had another one of those dreams.'

'You're calling me because you had a nightmare?' *It wouldn't be the first time*, One adds in his head.

'They're not nightmares, there's something different about them, I thought you'd at least listen to me.'

'Niente at this time of the morning a nightmare is a nightmare no matter how different.'

'Hey, thanks, I know not to bother calling next time.'

One sits up, best make the effort. 'No, Niente it's not like that, don't be stupid. You just woke me up.' He had been having such a good dream as well.

'Do you wanna meet up today?' Niente asks.

'I thought we were going to anyway.'

'Well, just checking. Okay, shall we meet at the Starbucks

on Camden High Street at 8:30?'

'8:30!' One repeats his voice high with shock. 'I wasn't expecting it to be that early.'

'Yeah but I'm awake, you're awake. Why bother waiting until later?'

*The only reason I'm awake is because of you,* One thinks but simply says 'Okay, I'll be there. 8:30 it is.'

'Cool,' Niente says, One can tell he is smiling. 'I'll start getting ready.' He hangs up.

One listens to the silence for a moment before closing his phone. He has known Niente for as long as he remembers; they have been through everything together. Always ready to support each other without question. Lately though Niente has been acting differently, small changes, a heavier pull towards the lure of his dreams. Niente is known to have his head in the clouds but now it seems as though he has been able to catch their tails, pulling them closer to reality. One smiles, 'determined', that is the word he is looking for.

He slides out of bed and makes his way to the bathroom. He looks in the mirror. Morning stubble and tired eyes look back. This is not the first time he has been awoken this early by Niente's dreams; they just seem to be becoming more frequent. One turns on the tap, filling the basin with warm water that he splashes onto his face. Another early start, another morning of trying to reassure Niente that everything is okay.

One returns to his room, picks up a pair of jeans from the floor and pulls them on. Unlike Niente, One is not too concerned about his image; as long as he looks vaguely presentable he is happy. He smiles, he knows Niente will be running around his flat trying to find something to wear, dressing himself in clothes that reflect his mood. Niente is one of those annoying people who can suit anything. *Bastard*, One says in his mind as he pulls on a clean t-shirt. The start of another day. Life rolling forward as normal.

The television screen continues to flicker, static still raining down from an unseen sky. The hand crumbles and the remote falls to the ground. The channel changes. The static remains the same.

Niente watches his reflection in the mirror. *Passable.* He turns to his side. In his rush it will have to do. Since finishing his call to One, he has showered, washed and scrubbed, left his three day old stubble the way it was and stumbled back into his bedroom to search for clothes to put on his naked frame. Living alone has its perks, you can spend a day without clothing and no one is there to complain, but at best it gives you space to breath, to think. Four walls to imprint your personality on the world. Houses like art galleries, put together by individuals, viewed by few.

So there he stands. Blue jeans, black t-shirt, tight fitting and plain. It suits his mood. He smiles as he looks, the male satisfaction to see the groin bulge in their jeans.

The television flickers quietly in the background, tuned to a dead channel. He tries to think when he last saw an image on its screen, the last time he saw the usual footage of traffic jams, accidents, all the insignificant news broadcasts to calm the masses. Much easier to report on that than the ongoing wars being fought in another country, more appealing than the money wasted on destroying what human hands had made. He should change the channel. He does not.

Niente sits in a chair and heats a spoon. Without tourniquet he jacks the needle into a vein. Plunger pushed he lets the euphoria burst through his system. He closes his eyes for a minute, but with no time to relax he gets to his feet with a sigh.

In his kitchen now, Niente swallows the contents of a glass of water. Picks up his keys and cigarettes from the side and takes one last tour of his home ensuring everything is turned off, shut down or closed. Satisfied he leaves, pulling on a jacket as he does. Time to face reality. Leave the sanctuary of the home for the humdrum of everyday life, to become a forgotten face in the crowd.

*Fuck, I hate winter,* Niente thinks as he steps out of his front door right into the gloom of the morning. The sun rising but not yet high enough to reach its bright beams down through the buildings to his level. Mid-February, cold but not raining. *That's something,* he supposes. He lets his feet guide him slowly, the street is deserted, everyone is either sat in endless traffic or locked underground in crowded carriages. He likes this street at this time of day. Silent, empty; the eyes of buildings watching his every move. Spectres of the past endlessly observing. London 2107, welcome to the future, it just looks like the past.

He pauses. Something is different. Feels different. Static shock in his eyes. He hits his head, refocuses, done. *What the fuck?* He turns full circle. The buildings look down at him, their eyes flickering blue lights from the television sets within. Flicker, flicker. The doors closed like dead mouths, brains rotting away out of sight. He shakes his head. The sky looks dead. The clouds moving in structure. Order in their chaos, like a sheet being pulled by invisible hands.

*When was the last time I watched something decent? When did I leave this city?* Head heavy, brain heavy. Headache. Scream. Pain. *Fuck, fuck, fuck.* That noise in the background, the low drone ebbing and flowing constantly.

He fumbles for his iPod, plugging the earphones into his ear. He presses play. Breathes. Music. Tracks on shuffle, the soundtrack of his life. Create a whole world in your mind and ignore the hundreds of disconnected noises around you. He rubs his hand down his face. The sky looks normal, the buildings just husks. A cigarette is pulled from its pack and worked into his mouth. Click, flame, inhale. He glances at his watch. 8am. He is going to be late.

Turn the corner and his numbed senses are swept along by the tidal wave of life.

One walks towards the Starbucks sign and through the door it crowns. Inside it is quiet.

'Coffee,' he says as the waitress approaches.

'What…'

He cuts over her with 'Coffee, just plain and simple coffee.' His voice irritable, he would have expected them to know his order by now, being a frequent visitor, but instead they continue to insist upon offering him frills to add to his drink. If he wanted a caramel macchiato with an extra shot and dash of cinnamon he would have joined the queues of the masses. He sighs, *so much choice for very little gain.*

'Plain coffee it is,' the barista summarizes before she scuttles off to make it. She returns and puts the cup in front of him.

As he places the money into her waiting hand, he glances

at the clock. 8:10. He is early but he needs this one extra caffeine hit to prepare him, to jolt his mind into action.

Table, sit, drink, wait.

Two coffees later, Niente arrives, casually breezing into the coffee shop. He orders a coffee before approaching the table and sitting down. They stare at each other in silence. Niente reaches for his coffee and drinks it. Lukewarm, slightly bitter, but drinkable. The cup is replaced and he resumes eye contact.

'Sorry I woke you up so early.'

One smiles. 'It's okay, I'm starting to get used to it.'

'There was something different about this one.'

'Different?' One questions, raising an eyebrow. 'How different?'

'It's hard to explain. They're beginning to feel so real. There's something in the air. Like everything is wrong. Can't you feel it?'

'And I guess you think that you've got a part to play in it?'

'I don't think, I kinda know.'

One laughs. 'All that certainty? Based on what? Something you heard in a dream? A vision? A "feeling"?'

Niente feels disappointed. If there was one person he thought he could trust to understand it was his best friend. 'Why so negative this morning?'

'You woke me up, herded me out of bed here just to tell me something we've already talked about. Do you expect me to act any different?'

'I don't expect anything from anyone, just a little understanding. This time is different. I feel different. Nothing feels "right". I don't expect you to believe me but try okay?'

One simply nods and picks up his coffee draining the cup. 'So what's changing?'

'Maybe nothing, maybe everything. Something needs to. I can't go on like this.'

'Are we talking about you or the world?'

'Both.'

'So this is Niente's personal quest to change the world?'

'What?' Niente shrugs off his coat. 'You know what, I don't even know myself anymore. I've just been thinking.'

'Anyway, regardless of what you feel, I don't think the Council's likely to allow any change. It's happy with how the country works, it won't allow someone like you to do anything to upset that.'

'I don't care about what the Council thinks. They're stagnant, swimming around in their own piss puddle. They care for no one but themselves, locked in their ivory tower they've kinda forgotten about us anyway.'

'That sounds revolutionary,' One jokes.

'Hardly, it's honest. Truthful. Think about it, when was the last time they showed their faces? I can't even remember what they look like. I can't even remember anything.'

One flicks his eyes to Niente's bare arms, taking in the fresh needle marks. 'Still using I see. Maybe that's where your answer lies.'

'It's got nothing to do with that.'

'Are you sober when you see these "visions"?'

'No, but…'

'Maybe you should just step back from it a bit.'

'It's got nothing to do with that, besides the woman said I'd need to keep using to see clearer.'

'What woman?'

'The dream woman.' Niente sighs, he knew instantly how that sounded before it even left his lips. In the silence he lets his eyes look around. The barista motionless behind the counter, blank eyes, vacant. The monotonous mumbles of other customers bleeding nonsense words into his head. He cannot understand anything. Things are being said but nothing is being meant. Claustrophobia surrounds him. He puts his head into his hand.

'Seriously, you need to slow down. You're fucking your head up. There's no going back from insanity. I'm concerned about you.'

Niente's hand hits the table. Silence. 'I'm fine. Everything in my head is no less fucked than it's ever been. That woman asked me to try and answer two questions. "When was the last time anything decent was on television, and when was the last time you left the city?" And you know what, I have no fucking clue on either of them.'

'You don't watch much television and you've had no need to leave. There's your answers. It's simple, you're looking too deep into it all.'

'How simple. How clever you are. That's it, got it in one. So what did you watch last night?'

'Can't remember.'

'Convenient. Okay, when was the last time you watched the news?'

One sits in silence for a moment. He sighs. 'And on that note, let's change the subject.' Easier to ignore than think about it. 'You going out later?'

'Yeah, I'm meeting up with Rose in a bit. Off out to the usual place. You wanna come along?'

'Nah, after last time I'll give it a miss. Best catch up on

sleep. It's my only day off this week so I'm gonna make the most of it.'

'Okay, no problem. *He's* probably going to be out tonight.' Niente's face screws up as though he wants to spit out something offensive.

'I thought you guys had sorted things out. Didn't know there was such a problem still.'

Niente sighs. 'There's always a problem, that's what the problem is. I can't do anything right no matter how I try. I keep my mouth shut and I'm sulking or moody; if I voice my concerns I'm ranting or trying to start an argument. I give up on hearing how he always has to walk on eggshells around me when he's the one causing the fucking problems.'

'Some things never change right? One rule for you, another for them. Why do you take so much shit?'

'Fuck knows. Always putting faith in others. That's gonna change. Trust me. No more shit taking.'

One laughs. He has heard that one before. Repeated and delivered like a well-rehearsed script. That is the one thing about Niente that never changes.

Niente smiles, knowing what his best friend is thinking. 'Don't say it and get the coffees in.'

# CHAPTER FOUR

Rose paces through to her kitchen. She is restless. Something does not feel right. She has the ability to pick up on these things; she has been doing it ever since meeting Niente. Some would think it was a gift but some days it feels like nothing more than a curse, more so recently. She touches the air in front of her. There is a change, a change in the unknown. Hard to pinpoint because there is no physical entity to pin it to. The air feels different. Some words have been spoken and the barriers are beginning to crumble. Times are changing, but for which direction she does not know.

Dreams have turned to nightmares. Visions, dark visions. The darkness engulfing everything. Shadows within shadows. Something has stirred and now it lays in wait. If only any of it made sense to her. *Time will tell,* she thinks, *no point wasting the present on fears of the unknown future.*

She looks at the clock on the wall. Niente would be arriving soon so she knows she had best get ready. Once he arrives it will be the usual series of events resulting in both of them being wasted. Tonight will be no exception; it has been a while since they last went out together.

Rose walks towards the bathroom, time for a shower, a quick clean before getting dirty again. Naked she pauses in front of the bathroom mirror, her eyes surveying her body. She rubs her hands against her slim form, tracing the curves of her structure. Placing her palms against her breasts, she cups them with her fingers. Not too big or too small. Her straight ginger hair falling just short of her shoulders. She smiles; she likes what she sees. She steps into the shower and lets the warm water rush over her.

Niente steps out of the shower; his second of the day. He catches his reflection in the mirror. He shudders. He has shaved since the morning but does not like what he sees. Hidden behind clothing he feels passable. Okay, sometimes a little awkward, but generally average. Naked, well, totally different. He averts his eyes, trying to keep his negativity at bay. He hates his figure, too skinny, awkward, disgusting. Others say otherwise but in his head it is a set in stone certainty. He hates it and nothing he has tried to do has been able to change either the way it looks or the way he feels. He pulls on his clothes and turns back to the mirror. His negative mind is locked. He looks stupid, shit, but that is just how it has got to be.

He picks up all the important objects he needs. Wallet, phone, ID, keys. Pulls a cigarette out from its packet and walks through the front door. It closes behind him.

Rose answers the door almost immediately as Niente knocks. He smiles and they embrace within a hug.

'I've opened a bottle of wine,' she says as he closes the door. 'I'll go pour us a glass each.'

Niente smiles. *Typical Rose and her wine.* He pats his pocket and pulls out the small bag within it. 'And look what I've brought along.'

Rose returns with the glasses and sees the bag Niente is

holding up to her. Seeing the six pills inside it she smiles. 'Niente you're the best. This is gonna be a fucking awesome night.'

'Tell me about it.' He opens the bag, taps out two of the pills, and swallows them with the wine he plucks from Rose's outstretched hand.

The club is packed. Filled with moving bodies and pounding music. The way it should be. The air weaving with lights and vibrations. They have just arrived, having worked their way through two entire bottles of wine. Buzzing, off their faces; arm in arm they paid and walked in. They look good together, always have, a suited match, complementing each other perfectly. Heads turn to look at them wherever they go; people confused as to how far their friendship actually extends. *Are they fucking or not?*

They have always been close; from the moment they first met at a funeral they connected. *There's something different about her*, Niente reflects about Rose. It is hard for him to imagine life without her being there. Love is what they feel, albeit not the physical kind most assume.

Niente casts his eyes around. Processing the scene. The same faces, same lustful glares. One naked, smacked out photo of him destroyed their fantasies and now they just go through the motions. Sycophantic faces hidden behind alcohol encrusted smiles. There was a point a while back when they had all been dressed in black, a sea of shadowed eyes; parasites infecting the latest trends with no identity to call their own. Then they got stuck on the bouffant hair and dirty shirts. Trends stopped changing, everyone paused on a new default.

'Drink?' Niente asks. Rose nods her head in agreement and they turn towards the bar. Drinks ordered and paid for they walk through the moving mass. Niente gulps down the contents of his glass, then it happens. A flash, a static burst blasting through his mind. The room groans, vision in slow motion. He hears Rose's voice, all slurred and distant. She is asking if he is okay. *No I bloody ain't.*

All around him darkness, the brightly coloured masses dulled to muted wasted colours. Jumping in waves, slow, pitiful. Swarms of so-called 'individuals' all huddled together like cockroaches. At one point in their lives they had all wanted to be movie stars and astronauts, but now they all herd together in their make up, living that life for a night before returning to their day jobs come the morning. *Herd mentality is the name of the game; let's all stick our figures down our throats like our size zero fashion queens.*

Disgust. Parasites, that is all they are. Leeching off each other. Using and abusing without care for anyone but themselves. Sucking each other off to add a notch to their sycophantic ego trips. The walls are lined with them. Naked men hung up like Christ whilst their mirror image places dead lips around their semi erect penises. A finger up the ass makes the host cum quicker into the receiver's mouth. Suck, swallow. The conveyor belt moves along. Suck, swallow. Niente rubs his face and averts his eyes.

*So is this what we have all become?* Faces in a crowd dropping pills and calling it difference? Is this what he is becoming? Are they a part of it, Rose and Niente? *If this is a trip, I'm seeing the world for what it really is.* A vision of parasites.

His attention is caught. There *he* is. *Him,* Niente's so called 'boyfriend'. He feels nothing for him but empty. Any feelings dead and buried. His boyfriend, the one who constantly sucks his creativity, his hopes and dreams, his happiness. A leech bleeding Niente dry. There he dances, body to body against a stranger. *He's welcome to do what he wants,* Niente hears a voice say in his head. *He's nothing to me.*

The room melts, the walls bleeding away to nothing. The cast crack out of their skin revealing their true parasitic form. The flashing strobe lights flicker dully, everyone fades to black except the writhing figure of his boyfriend. Shadows dancing around their queen. Disconnected from the herd Niente can see her. Stood by the bar she raises her glass at him in acknowledgement before taking a drag on her cigarette. She mouths the word 'Parasites' as she exhales.

*I know you want me, you say you need me but then you'll just throw me away. You want to use me, abuse me and leave nothing in return. Well come on then, fucking use me, you parasites come abuse me.*

*Creatures without direction endlessly seeking meaning.*

# CHAPTER FIVE

Niente opens his eyes. He is lying down on a sofa, he knows where. He is back at Rose's flat; he has been here in this position so many times. This time is different. Everything is so fucking different. *What is happening to me?* The vision he saw at the club playing on his mind, flashing back before his eyes. A sea of cockroaches, a mass of leeches, a vision of parasites. The melting pot of mankind's ethics. *Lost souls now govern the Earth.*

*What's causing it, these visions?* he thinks. *It's not the alcohol; it's not the drugs.* All throughout the day he had seen glimpses of a world he has grown to detest. A couple of 'trips' and he has these new life choices. He rubs his face. *No, it's not the substances I'm using; they only give me the ability to see everything clearly.* Only when you are truly disconnected can you see without blinds.

He turns over onto his side and pushes his body up. Sat with his head in his hands the world swirls. Twists and turns. His nose hurts, his head heavy. The night had obviously continued without his mind noticing. No doubt Rose will fill him in on all the details when she chooses to surface from her room. *What I need to do is think clearly and plan.* Or he could simply do what he normally does, go with the flow and let the journey take him wherever it chooses. The goal will be reached regardless, if it is his destiny to reach it. Wait until your piece is played and then rise for the occasion. That is what he has done all his life; he has got the scars to prove it.

*Stand up and walk*, that is what he tells his brain and it obeys as usual, well almost. He staggers into the kitchen and pours himself a glass of water from the tap. *So what the fuck happened last night?* Does he really want to know? *Maybe not.*

Second glass of water drunk, he returns to the sofa carrying the third. His mind is blank, he does not feel the need to think about anything other than the hunger pains in his stomach, nor does he really want to. No point pondering on the unknown. As he sits, his stomach rumbles as if on cue; he is not in the mood to get up again, he will just wait until Rose is up, then they can eat together whilst she fills in the blanks. *Kill two birds with one stone.* He smiles picturing the image.

From the side of the sofa he pulls out the wooden box Rose keeps her rig in. *She won't mind.* He unpacks a fresh needle. Powder, water, lighter. Mix, suck, prick, push. Breathe. He lies back down, his eyes close. He falls asleep.

*There.*

The land stretches before his eyes, a silhouette against a blood red sky; large black drops of rain pouring down like ink spills. The noise, so much noise. Explosions, planes, screaming, the running feet of a thousand panicked people, all merging into a beautiful cacophony. Niente watches from the sky, god-like and disconnected. So much pain and anger. His eyes close. *What did they all expect? A god of peace and love to just sit and watch his angst-ridden children destroy his creation?*

Through the darkness behind his eyelids the noise intensifies. He feels the push of people crowding around him, swarming past like water around a rock. He looks. Stood on the street of the silhouette city, shadow figures running; screaming wraithlike shapes flowing through in fear. So dark, the sky burning red with fire. He tries to listen, to feel but the noise is too much. Too many voices screaming in pain. The voices of men, women and children all merge into one voice. The cry of humanity to which no one is listening.

The crowd pushes him forward. A sea of the unknown, no faces, no eyes, no features; he is just one face in a thousand. He looks at his arms, stained black from the rain, almost lost to the shadows. His individuality fading. He feels their pain, the smell of their fear, the depth of their anger, the loss in their confusion. One collected group, one collected goal to survive. He opens his mouth to scream, to release his emotion but nothing comes. A silent scream. Sometimes pain is too great to make a noise.

The rain continues to fall, faster and thicker. Painting the world with its darkness, covering over the scene, shielding it from sight. The blood from divine abandon, it washes over him; the last of his colour hidden, he succumbs to the cold. So many voices screaming into the dark.

*Present.*

Two voices talking. The sound of clattering plates, the smell of cooking. He opens his eyes again. He has no idea of how long he has been asleep. The voices in the kitchen laugh. One is definitely Rose, the other an unclear male mumble. Niente guesses Rose got lucky last night, she usually does, especially in gay bars. He hears the front door open and the stranger leave. He does not bother to look or acknowledge him; it is not like he will see him again. The door closes,

Rose's footsteps return into the room and stop at the head of the sofa.

'You're awake ain't you?' she asks.

'Yeah, so who was he?'

'Don't you remember? We met him last night after your argument. Although we were both pretty wasted so I wouldn't be surprised if you don't.'

Niente sits up and smiles. 'And I wouldn't be surprised if you only learnt it this morning when you woke up next to him.'

Rose laughs. 'That's pretty much what happened.'

'Big cock? Good in bed?'

'I guess a little above average, and I can't remember. Luckily he was hot.' They both laugh. 'You okay though?'

'Yeah, why wouldn't I be?'

'Erm, your argument.'

Niente frowns. 'What argument?' *Do I really want to know?* he adds as an afterthought in his head.

'You and Anthony, in the club. You saw him with some guy and he tried to rub it in your face but got all pissy when you didn't care.'

Niente gets to his feet. 'That wouldn't surprise me.'

'It was pretty bad. You were right up in his face screaming at one point.'

'He'll get over it. I already have.' The usual routine, his boyfriend always trying to put him down, always trying to compete, always wanting to be better.

'Oh my god! Niente you really don't remember.' Rose laughs. 'You ended it with him. Dumped him then told him to fuck off.'

Niente laughs. 'Really? Oops. Shame I don't remember it.

That would have been a good memory to keep.'

'Yeah, you should have seen his face.' Rose sounds satisfied, she never liked his boyfriend. 'It was the last thing he was expecting.'

Niente takes his empty glass into the kitchen and fills it. Rose is in the process of cooking breakfast. Sausages, bacon and eggs. An old classic but always the best. 'So that makes me single then?' He drinks. 'Me single and you, well, the same.'

Rose enters the kitchen, hugs Niente in passing and proceeds to serve up the food onto plates. 'What happened to you last night? You suddenly changed. Your mood just switched.'

Niente takes a plate and returns to sit on the sofa. He does not want to talk about it. 'You know, Rose, I really don't know how you do it. Always finding some straight guy in whatever gay bar we end up in.'

'How do you know he was straight? He could have been bi.'

'If he'd swung both ways, I wouldn't have woken up on the sofa would I? Especially if what happened with Anthony was as bad as you said.'

'Maybe if the night had just been fueled by the usual plenty of alcohol and narcotics.' She pauses. 'But there was also your little mood trance.' She is not going to let it drop.

'I was just a bit wasted, had a little trip. I dunno, everything feels different, what with all these visions and then that. Something is changing.'

'You feel it too then?' She sounds relived. 'Thought I was going crazy.'

'I think we're both going crazy, we're rubbing off on

each other.' Niente laughs and eats a mouthful of food. 'I tried talking to One about it yesterday, he didn't seem too concerned about it. Says it's all down to the drugs.'

'He would though, what were you expecting?'

'I dunno, someone to just listen.'

'I take it he said to cut down.'

'Yeah.'

'Are you?'

'No. One of my visions told me continuous use would help me see things more clearly.'

'Hmm.'

'What? Don't you start.'

'I'm not, really I'm not.'

They finish their food in silence.

'What are we going to do today?' Niente asks once both plates are empty.

'I dunno, don't have anything to do.'

'Well, I don't want to be locked up inside all day so I'm gonna go for a walk, get out and about. You can tag along if you want.'

'Okay.' She smiles. 'Now I've got to decide what to wear.'

'Take it you'll be an hour then?' Niente jokes.

'Well, after this I won't care.' She nods to the box.

Niente smiles. They both do.


*There.*

Mind snaps back to a scene. A body being pulled along by the shadows surrounding him. The pain, their pain, the world's pain echoing through his senses. The silent scream.

Focus, he tries to will his brain out of the collective mind. Focus on the scene, the tall factory building rising out of the fog, its tall chimneys churning out thick black smoke, which snakes into the air before dispersing into leaden clouds that spit their burden down onto the earth. The snow falls, grey and dirty. Herded inside he breaks free. Forces himself away from the masses and escapes down a silent staircase to his left, a shadowy void descending into darkness. Step after step the silence fills his head. Silence. Blissful numbed senses. Momentary. A click followed by a low hiss. A door slides open in the fabric of the air in front of him. He steps through.

The scene changes. Niente stands in the middle of a warehouse. Naked bulbs swinging dimly in the air above his head. Their dirty orange glow barely illuminating his surroundings. That noise. The twisted warble, the sound his ears have come to dread. Its heartbeat fills his ears. His head hurts. Eyes, static burst then focus. In the shadows lurk shadows. He steps forward and they emerge from the darkness. Humanoid forms thrashing about on the floor, trying in vain to pull the gas masks free from their faces. Their skin a fungus grey covering pulled taught over their bones. Frantic movements. Silver tears running down their faces. One gets to his feet and staggers towards him. No face, no eyes. Just empty sockets and their tears. The figure's head jolts back when the tube leading from the mask reaches its end. Anchored a few feet from him, Niente hears its whisper in his head. A pleading voice, a language unknown to him.

'I don't understand you,' Niente offers.

The figure's hands rise. Reaching towards him. The whisper continues in desperation.

He feels a tear fall from his eye. 'I don't understand.'

The rumble of a generator drowns out everything. From

where they fade into the distance the clear tubes fill with a luminous green gas. The prostrate forms struggle more, thrashing with the fear of an ending. The one standing before him drops its arms. The gas creeps the last inches of its tube. Resigned to its fate it stands. Its silver tears turn a putrid green and its head withers away like ageing fruit. The form crumbles to the floor. Thud. The generator stops, the gas retracts. Nothing moves. Nothing lives. No post trauma twitches. Nothing lies as still as a corpse.

Footsteps. A man in a stiff black uniform approaches, his shoes clicking against the concrete floor. He talks as he approaches but the words muffle against Niente's ears and he does not understand. He does not get it. 'What have you done?' he screams at the uniformed figure. 'What the fuck have you done?'

The officer looks at Niente through dead eyes. 'What have I done?' he says, his voice sharp, cutting. 'What did *you* do?' His hands grip Niente's face. 'When you watch in silence, pray your dreams will come.' He throws him onto the ground.

'I didn't do anything,' Niente shouts.

The officer jumps on top of him, pinning Niente to the floor with his knees. Leaning into Niente's face, he spits a cupful of black blood into it. It sticks like tar. Hands slip around Nietne's throat. The officer's mouth moves. 'When you stand in silence, pray your dreams will come.'

# CHAPTER SIX

The wind blows all around them, the train approaching quickly. Rose had woke Niente from his nap. She was wearing her usual attire. Black leggings, short tartan shirt and long black coat, her ginger hair pulled back into a ponytail. They had had another hit before they left and here they are. Underground. Midday and busy. The train slips into the platform. Its doors open and they step on. Standing in the middle of the carriage. The doors close and they are ejaculated from the station.

They stand in silence. Niente's eyes scan the crowd. One guy looks at him. Staring. His face familiar. Niente feels like he should know him but he does not. It feels to him like their paths are destined to cross at some point in the future, or maybe they were meant to have already but did not. Memories. Memories of that face in his head and yet he does not have a clue as to why or how.

'See what you do to me?' the stranger says, half naked, his hardened cock stretching the fabric of his boxer shorts. 'Let's have sex.'

'Okay,' Niente replies simply, the towel falling from his waist as they begin to make out.

They fuck on someone else's bed. Mad, rampant thrusts. Niente pushing deep into the stranger. Slam, slam, slam.

They have been waiting to do this for so long and now the passion is released it refuses to stop until they lay spent on each other, the thick sludge of cum squashed between their naked flesh. Deep breathing. They are late. Niente's phone rings, it is his boyfriend, Anthony. He answers, speaks. Shower. Regrets? Zero. Remorse? None.

'Niente?' Rose's voice next to him.

Niente's attention snaps back. His hard cock pressing against his jeans, he looks and sees that it is hidden, no one can see, *good*. 'Yeah?'

'You zoned out into your own little world. Where are we headed?'

'Dunno.' he shrugs. His eyes return to the stranger, he is still looking. Still staring, his eyes show the same recognition as Niente's.

Lying in front of a fireplace, open flame crackling. Side by side, naked. Post fuck and tired. It is all too real. It is all too true.

'Niente.'

'What?' Niente answers, impatience in his voice.

'Are you okay?'

'Yeah, I just keep zoning out like you said.'

The train stops and the stranger gets to his feet, he walks towards them. They watch. Looking Niente straight in the eyes the stranger says, 'I love you.'

Niente's mouth opens and he feels himself blush. A staccato of staggered words stumble from his lips. The stranger walks away and out of the train. Doors close, they move away. His haunting final look stuck in Niente's mind. *I love you too.*

'What a weirdo,' Rose states with a laugh.

Niente looks her full in the face. 'I know him.'

'Do you? When? Err, how?'

'I dunno but I know him. Like we should have been. That sounds weird no?' *What the fuck is happening?*

'Are you sure you're okay?' She places her hand on his arm.

'Yeah.' The strangers face in his mind. *Why is it still there?* If he could, he would cry.


Niente and Rose walk out of Tottenham Court Road station, the streets filled with people. A constant, streaming mass of moving faceless people. Their eyes meet and they melt into the crowd hand in hand. They flow down the road towards a destination of nowhere.

Rose stops suddenly. Niente does the same. 'What's wrong?' he asks.

'I dunno.' She does not move.

The crowd moulds around them, splitting and reforming; their journeys unfaltering. Rose rubs her eyes. She looks. She rubs again.

'Can't you see it?' she questions.

Niente looks. 'See what?'

'The flames, the fire burning above their heads.'

'Whose heads?'

'People's.' She does not look at him; her eyes too busy flicking around. 'Not everyone's, only a few. Two colours. Red. Blue.' She points out an approaching male, he walks towards them smartly, his suit creased in all the right places.

Above his head a red flame flickers, floating in the air above his crown. 'He's red. The girl next to him is the same. That baby in the pram is blue yet his mum has nothing.'

Niente looks but sees nothing, just normal people going about their casual business. 'Are you okay?'

'You can't see it? Niente, it's beautiful. Little flickers of colour, like candles. Two blues together, a red watching us and frowning.' A smile crosses her lips.

'Auras?'

'No, this is different. I dunno, it's random, disconnected. I, I don't know. I don't get it.' She looks at Niente, the smile quivering from her lips. 'You're red.'

'What?'

'You've got a flame burning above your head. It's red.'

Niente looks around him. No flames, just people. He stares into Rose's eyes. Something lurks in them. Something he has never seen. A small dot of emptiness deep in her soul. 'Are you sure you're okay?'

'I'm perfect. This is amazing. It's like I've finally trained my gift. We said things were changing, maybe this is part of that.'

'So this is all new? I hate to sound like One, but given what's happened today I think it could be the drugs.'

'No, I remember seeing a flash a few months ago. Feeling like certain people are hot or cold, red or blue. But visually, no, that is new.' She rubs her eyes. 'What do you reckon this could mean?'

'I dunno.' Niente grabs her hand and pulls her forward, beating their way through the crowd without care, knocking past everyone. Ignoring the glares and grunts he leads the way to Soho Square. Away from the noise they sit on a bench in silence. *What the fuck is happening?* Niente thinks.

His eyes scan their surroundings; a few people are littered around on the remaining benches, on the grass, or walking, their yapping dogs running around gleefully after thrown sticks. He looks at Rose. 'Still see it?'

She nods vaguely without looking.

'So, what do you reckon it is? A sign?'

A shrug.

'Oh, so what?  Now it's the silent treatment? What have I done now?'

'You believe me don't you?'

'Given what I've seen I can't not.' He puts his arm around her shoulders. 'Maybe we are going that little bit crazy.'

She barks a laugh. 'I don't like it. I don't want to see all this. This is your world.' She tilts her head to look at him, her eyes wet. 'I don't want to see all this.'

They hug. From over Niente's shoulder Rose's gaze is drawn towards the woman sat staring at them from across the park. A cigarette is pulled from her lips by one hand whilst the other holds a glass. She exhales slowly. The darkness flickers above her like storm clouds.


The image remains in her mind all day. Locked there like a Polaroid pinned to the wall of her consciousness. It still sits in her head, repeating in slow motion. Haunting her every thought. That face staring at her holding her best friend, the eyes burying into her. Rose had felt a crawling sensation over her skin as she had been unable to tear her eyes away from the old woman. Then there was the darkness, the swirling cloud of black above her head, stretching out towards them. She could sense it watching her with disgust, could feel it trying to reach out and touch her. Then with a nonchalant shrug of the shoulders, the woman had taken a final draw of her cigarette, dropped its corpse to the ground and crushed it out under foot as she got up and walked away, taking the shadows with her.

*What could it mean?* Rose thinks. With a shaking hand she lifts the wine glass off the table and drowns its red contents. Should she tell Niente she saw her? It could only be the woman he saw haunting him. *But if she is just a dream vision, why could I see her? Why did Niente not notice her?*

Bottle fills glass. She washes down two blue pills of Valium and sits back on the sofa. Calm; calm flowing through her with its warm fuzz. Her veins breathing sighs of relief with every pump, pushing the sensation like little blown kisses towards her heart.

*Can dreams manifest in reality?* An involuntary smile cuts across her lips. *Maybe it is the drugs.* Her hand cradles her head as she leans forward again. Rising slowly to her feet, she walks to the bathroom.

She looks in the mirror. Tired eyes look back. A splash of water on her face and her tired eyes still look back. A flash of red above her head. A frown. The door closes; she sees it out of the corner of her eye before the lights switch off, plunging the room into darkness.

A hum, a dirty hiss like static. Her eyes adjust to the gloom, somehow absorbing light from nowhere to enable a murky vision. She watches her reflection. The mirror rippling like water, she reaches forward and her hand disappears into the arm of her other self. She goes to pull back but with a cruel smile her other self drags her through. Gripping at her hair, pulling her head first into its world.

Rose screams, her noise exploding like bubbles of oxygen underwater. Rising to deposit the sound elsewhere. Anywhere but where she needs it.

Half way between worlds she hears it, ripping through the silence. Her phone. Energy. With all her might she fights back. Pulling herself to reality. Stumbling to the floor she grabs her mobile phone. It is Niente. She answers. 'Niente help me.'

'Hello?'

'Niente, get round here now,' she shouts, her words dead around her.

'Rose, are you okay?'

'No I'm fucking not. I need you.'

'Rose?'

'Niente, can't you fucking hear I'm in fucking trouble?'

'Rose? Hello? Are you there?'

'Niente?' Confusion in her voice. 'Niente?'

'Hello? Rose? Stop playing games.'

She sobs. 'I'm not. Just help me. Dear God come and save me.'

'Rose, your phone's fucked. I'm coming round; I left something there. If you can get this message then be ready for me.'

Rose croaks. 'Niente…'

'I love you Rose.'

A static squeal.

'Rose, what the fuck?'

'Rose isn't here.' A new voice says. Deep, dead. Dark. The line cuts before a reply.

A burning; she looks, the phone melting in her hand. It drops to the floor covered in blood, her blood. Shards of glass lay littered around her. She sees the shattered mirror as she runs from the room.

The flat burns a dull orange. The naked bulbs of the lights swinging from the ceiling like pitiful orbs. Thick pipes run along the floor, clear, filled with a green gas. Rose slams into the bedroom and falls against the closed door.

*What's happening?* she wonders, her fingers tap silently against the carpeted floor, drumming out morse code signals to remind herself she only has to sit it out, that it is only a bad trip. *Niente will be around soon and everything will then be okay. Just keep calm and remember to breathe.*

Footsteps outside the door. Pacing up and down. Rose turns and gets onto her knees an peers through the keyhole below the door's handle. She hears the mournful wail of babies crying in their dead mother's arms before she sees them. Suckling at the decaying tit for the remains of the rancid milk within it. The deafening screams as they fall into the jaws of the awaiting pit ball, hungry for any morsel that comes its way. With a sickening crunch, the jaws snap shut and the dog falls down, its lower body mutating, evolving. Soon the bipedal beast is clawing at the door, blood slavering from its jowls; eyes red with lust.

The door buckles behind her. Rose jumps up and runs to the bed. The slap catches her unawares and she stumbles onto it and turns.

'The boy is mine,' the woman says, taking a drag of her cigarette. 'I know you can feel it too but this is not your game my dear.' A swig of vodka.

'Who are you?'

'It matters little at this moment. The gates are opening and you my dear will not undermine that by neglecting your role.'

'Role?'

'You and him are one of a kind. But you need to tear his heart out and break him'

'Never.'

'Did I say it was an option?'

'Did I?'

'Listen lady.' A sharp drag on the cigarette. 'Answer the next question. What is the date?'

'What?'

The doorbell rings.

'What is the date?' A swig from the glass.

'I'll scream, that'll be Niente.'

'Scream all you want my dear.' She smiles sweetly, cruelly. 'The boy remains mine.'

# CHAPTER SEVEN

'I'm really worried about Rose,' Niente says as he sits across from One. They sit opposite each other inside a Costa next to Mornington Crescent Underground station. One had finished his night shift at University College Hospital to find Niente waiting outside the hospital for him. Together they had walked down Hampstead Road in an awkward silence.

'I'm telling you it's all that crap you are pumping into your veins.' One looks at his coffee. 'I'm in here pretty much every morning and still they don't know what I drink.'

'Oh cheers for that,' Niente spits. 'I'm telling you this and all you give a shit about is your coffee. Don't you get bored coming in here?'

'No, habit, and sorry it's not a bloody Starbucks,' One says sarcastically. 'And with regards to Rose, well, if you are fucking up you brought it upon yourselves. I warned you.'

'Thanks, thanks a fucking lot.'

'Well, you should both do something with your lives. Get a job.'

'What? In this stinking city? What is there? There's nothing new, no new scenes, no new buildings, no jobs, no hope. The city is dying on its feet and no one cares or notices. One, I can't get what that woman said out of my head, it's like a seed germinating. There's nothing on TV, and no one can tell me what they watched last night. It's like everything is on pause. Can you honestly say you feel like your life is going anywhere?'

'Well—'

'Happy with it?'

'No, but—'

'Then why don't you change it?'

'What, and end up in the gutter? I am content and there's no need to change it.'

'You're a drone, an ant, nothing but part of the system. You've changed One, you really have. Where's the spark you had? The direction?'

One slams down his coffee mug. 'Well, I hate to break it to you Niente but whilst you're out running around seeing imaginary flames and age shifting women, some of us are actually trying to have a normal existence.

'What do you want from me? For me to say that everything is okay? To be worried about Rose's self-induced delirium? Well I can't. Yeah it's sad she's got herself into a state but it's her own fault.'

'She saw the same fucking woman that I did. She's feeling it too and you pretend that you can't. Great, thanks. Keep your support, we don't need it.' Niente gets to his feet.

'Niente, don't go.'

Niente leans into One's face and spits. 'Go fuck yourself. I'll make you see I'm right and you'll regret it.' He straightens up and heads to the door. At it he turns. 'Hey guys,' he shouts to everyone. 'Can anyone tell me the date?'

Confused murmurs fill the air, everyone shifts uncomfortably in their seats, averting their eyes from Niente. No answer comes. As Niente opens the door he looks at One. 'Can you?'

The door slams behind him.

*There.*

Her eyes open, vision clears, brain focuses through the fog of darkness. Snow. Black snow. It swirls above her like fragments of nightmares falling like ash. Her brain whirls, clicks, fails to comprehend.

*Where am I?* she thinks. The pat down. *Clothes intact, wait, no, no clothes. What?*

Her eyes flick down, her naked form lying in the black snow. Ebony snow. Cold. A needle hanging from her arm. She pulls it out, a tear of blood runs from tiny entry wound, a scene shot in black and white with one small burst of red. The needle feels heavy in her hand; she lets it drop. It shatters against the soft floor, its delicate sound echoing out in the silence.

Forcing herself up to her feet, Rose looks around in the dim light. She rubs her eyes. The vision remains the same. *What the fuck?*

'Welcome to my world.' The voice comes from behind her. Familiar. Her heart stops for a second. The voice continues, 'Do you like what you see?'

'Why can't you just fuck off?' Rose screams as she spins round. No one stands behind her. Just an expanse of darkness extending into nothing.

'I told you why,' the voice whispers into her ear.

Rose turns, next to her stands a girl, although short in height, her maturing face makes Rose feel like the girl must be at least twelve years old. In one hand a glass of vodka, the other a cigarette. She raises the cigarette to her lips and inhales. Pauses. Exhales. A grim smile on her lips.

'Who are you?' Rose asks.

'That does not matter at this point.'

'I think it does.'

'Why? In the end, at the end of it all, all names are meaningless.'

'What?'

'Did you find the answer to my question? Or did you just shy away under the influence of your drugs.'

'Don't start that bullshit as well.'

'Date?'

'What?'

A sip of vodka. 'What day is it?'

'Erm.' Rose thinks. She does not know. Each day rolling and merging into a blur. 'I can't remember.'

'Cannot or will not?'

'I just have no clue, there's nothing wrong with that.'

'Are you convinced on that?'

'Oh fuck off.' Rose pushes the girl to the floor. She falls in slow motion. She hits the ground in an explosion. Hundreds of files erupt from where the girl had fallen. They fly into the air and swarm chaotically around Rose.

*Nothing.*

The scene stops. Lights out. Darkness. No garden of snow. No light. Silence. Infinity. Floating in limbo. Lost and alone. Rose screams but nothing leaves her lips. Dead zone. A pinprick of light in the distance draws her attention. She runs towards it. Runs as quickly as her numbed legs can carry her.

The light grows with each step. Engulfs her.

*Wake up.*

Her eyes snap open. Lying on her own bed, Rose breathes a sigh of relief. Her heart racing, she tries to calm herself.

An elderly face blows smoke into Rose's face. 'The boy is mine.'

Rose screams.

*Reality.*

Rose sits up sharply. Her racing heart pounding within her fragile frame. The needle falls from her arm and clatters clumsily to the floor. She jumps out of bed. Her foot stamps on it. The needle cuts through and she stumbles forward.

Flat on the floor she gathers her thoughts. *Just a dream. A nightmare, another in the usual series. Try to calm down. Awake and safe. Nothing can touch me.*

She pulls the syringe out of her foot and walks into the bathroom where she splashes water over face. Her reflection stares brokenly back at her, its eyes accusing. What has she become? Her head empty, heavy. Feeling like it is about to snap. Shatter. Tear apart into some new mentality.

*Shit,* she thinks. *I'm really fucking up.*

In the living room the television flickers on a dead channel. Its static rain sending her cold. Reminding her of the dream. Ash falling from the sky on the wings of angelic abandon.

Finger on the remote, she turns the television off, then throws an ashtray through its screen.

The doorbell rings. Niente has arrived. She is still naked.

Sat in McDonalds, Niente and Rose stare out at the stalls that line Chapel Market. From their position by the window they watch the bustling street in silence. They had walked from Rose's flat, down Liverpool Road with a distance between them, their shoulders drooped and eye lines focused down at the ground moving before their feet; looking up in quick flashes to see if the other was looking at them, always timing it wrong and as a muted conversation topic ground to an end, the space between the next grew longer, awkward, resulting in the tense silence that lingered over their table.

'There's got to be a logical reason for it,' Niente says suddenly, turning his head to look at Rose.

'Yeah, we've done too much we've cracked.'

'Surely we wouldn't see the same things though. I just don't get it. What do all these visions mean?'

'I'm still sticking with what I said. We've finally gone and lost it.' She forces a dry smile.

'I'm worried about you.'

'I'm fine.' Her bloodshot eyes say otherwise. 'I just need a break.'

'A break?'

'Yeah, a break from everything. To come down into the real world for a bit.'

Niente takes a bite of his burger. He says nothing.

'I need to stay away from you.'

'What?'

'Whilst I'm around you, there is danger.'

'Danger from a vision? She's harmless.'

'I'm in danger. My sanity. This is going to tear us apart. I can't let that happen. I won't. We need a break.'

'We can get through this. We'll help each other.'

'I can't do it. I can't force you to stop. I know you don't want to.'

'Who says?'

'Well, do you?'

'No.'

'Then there's your answer.' She breaks eye contact and looks at her bruised arms. 'I don't even know when I'm using anymore. It's routine, forgettable. I can't do it. I can feel my mind snapping.' She taps her head. 'Something in here doesn't feel right.'

Niente taps his head. 'Something in here has never felt right, but it feels like it is finally making sense, even if it's in a fucked up way.'

'I can't help you. I just want my old life back. I can't have that if I'm with you.'

'What's that meant to mean?'

'You. That's what it means. Your personality is too strong. It sucks everything towards it. I'm lost in your shadow.'

'Are you saying I've forced you to be this way?'

'I knew you'd react like that.'

'How the fuck am I meant to react?'

'Niente, you gave me my first hit. You let me into your world and have kept me there. I'm the one who you made understand. I can't exist in there anymore; I don't know how you do it, but really I can't. Anything you say doesn't matter anyway.' She reaches for her coat. 'I've made up my mind.'

'You can't leave until we've finished this conversation.'

'I need some air.'

Niente grabs his coat. 'We'll talk on the way then.'

'Niente.'

'I'm not leaving it like this.' He rises to his feet. 'Come on then.' He shrugs on his coat and walks to the door. Rose follows quietly.

The street is deserted as they walk down it in silence. Everyone locked in an office or shop. Life as commanded by others. They walk with space between them for the first time ever.

'Can you still see those flames?' Niente asks after a while.

Rose nods her reply.

'Any more thoughts on them?'

'I don't want to think about them in all honesty.'

Niente stops walking. Rose stops a few paces ahead but does not turn. 'So you just choose to ignore it all. How very easy of you.'

'It doesn't concern you.'

'So that's how it is. No talking, just closing a door.'

'Niente, I'm tired. I can't do this anymore. I just need to be left alone.'

'But you said we'd talk as we walk.'

She turns to him finally. 'No, you said that.'

Niente bites back his tears. 'It can't end like this.'

'It hasn't ended. It's a break. Just give me a few days to myself. Is that too much to ask for?'

'No.'

'Thank you.'

'Wait here for me, one second. I need to buy some cigarettes. Say you'll do that at least.'

'Okay.'

'Promise?'

'Promise.'

Niente turns and runs back down the road to the shop. He looks before entering. He sees Rose's figure walking in the opposite direction. He watches her walk away in silence.

The cigarettes are placed on the counter. Niente hands over the money, picks up the pack of twenty and leaves.

As he walks from the shop his attention is grabbed by the newspapers on the rack. He pauses and looks across each imprint. He feels sick. His brain unable to comprehend what he sees. He has walked past so many newspaper stands and never bothered to look. He wishes he had.

He rereads the date on the newspaper he holds in his hand. It reads the same as all the others. 23 July 2104.

Three years ago.

# CHAPTER EIGHT

*There.*

The snow falls before her eyes. Black flakes. Without thinking Rose knows where she is. She takes a moment to adjust to the scene. It is different. She looks around, when she turns to look behind her a frown creases across her face. A factory looms through the twilight before her, dark and oppressive. Remembering, she checks her body. This time she is fully clothed, except for her bare feet. She finds a packet of cigarettes and works one out, she brings it to her lips and lights it with a lighter she finds in her back pocket. The factory pulls her attention and she walks towards it.

Through the mist and falling snow she sees the tall chimneys standing like sentinels at the heart of the building. Their tops pumping out huge clouds of black. Giant black cigarettes with their cancerous smoke. The falling flakes are not snow she realises, but ash from the cloud of darkness that surrounds the chimney tops. *Dreaming,* she thinks, reminding herself. *It's just a dream.*

A footstep behind her, faint, distant. She freezes. Voices, muffled voices approaching. Her eyes flick from left to right, the landscape is barren, devoid of all life and offering no place for shelter. No escape but forward towards the cover of the factory. Its essence pulling her towards it with a promise of safety. She counts to three then runs. Runs through the high gates that are connected to the high brick walls that surround the building, their tops lined with barbed wire. The gates lead into an empty courtyard. She runs across it, her bare feet slapping against the cobbled stone floor. She hears the shadows running behind her, swooping in to capture her. Her feet power on, propelling her to her destination without looking back. She blinks. She disappears.

Another blink and she is inside. *What the fuck?* Her eyes adjust to the gloom. She stands in a narrow corridor, the whitewashed walls only inches from her skin. Naked bulbs above her cast a dull hue of orange over the scene. Bright enough to see, dark enough to not. They sway in an invisible wind, causing the shadows in front of her to stretch and contract, to show and hide. She sees scattered items of clothing: a shoe, a hat, a pair of glasses. All discarded without order across the floor. Thick translucent pipes crawl along the tops of the walls without indication of their flow of direction.

She decides to walk forward and not turn her body in the other direction. Step after step. The glasses snap and shatter under her feet, she grimaces as the glass scratches against her skin. The fragile sound disturbs the shadows and they retreat from her like a swarm of cockroaches as the lights brighten. She picks up her pace and rushes down the corridor. The lights flicker and dim again. A door opens ahead of her. Her feet do not stop and she runs through. It slams shut before she has chance to turn.

Another room lit by naked bulbs. Another room of shadows. A noise rumbles out from nowhere. A dark noise, dirty and twisted. It causes her heart to beat in time with it. Made one with the heartbeat of the darkness. As it grows in volume the shadows animate, pulling away from the corners they approach, growing into people, thin people, emaciated and featureless except for their eyes; gas masks connected to their faces, sown on with wire, their eyes pulled open with hooks. Their advance hindered as the pipe that feeds their masks reaches its limit. They hold their hands out to her. Begging, pleading in a muffled language she does not understand.

'I don't know what you're saying,' Rose says aloud. 'I don't know how to help you.'

The figure in front beckons her closer. Pleading with its eyes. She reaches for its hand. It grabs her. She screams.

Pulled into the crowd they tear at her clothes, ripping them off her body and throwing them into the air. She tries to run but they grip on to her with cold fingers, pushing her to her knees. The crowd parts and the figure that first beckoned her approaches. She realises they are all naked. She can feel the penis of the one holding her on her knees digging into her back, rubbing greasily against her spine. She screams again, it is silenced by the erection of the one she had trusted.

She gags but the figure continues to thrust frantically inside her mouth. Thrust, thrust, thrust. Nothing. Its body spasms and goes limp. The emaciated figure falls backwards, spitting a load as its cock leaves her throat. The cum lands lazily on the ground beside the twitching body.

All around her the figures fall. Stumbling to their knees, trying to rip the masks from their faces. Trying to escape the green gas that now fills the tubes, being pumped into their lungs. They die in silence and she lies amongst their corpses.

A static burst, and her eyes refocus. She is alone. No corpses; just empty gas masks lying in pools of black blood having been pulled from the faces of their owners. Her breathing shallow panicked gasps receding into normality. Another burst of static flashes across her vision. Refocus. Rose sees a door in the wall opposite, off center and open. Light flooding in from within. She is still alone. Still naked. Still can taste it in her mouth.

She pushes herself to her knees and re-evaluates the scene. She broadens her shoulders as she straightens her back, turning her hands into fists as she raises her arms in front of her face. Nothing. Rose slowly lowers her arms. Nothing. Confused, she stands fully and turns full circle. Empty space and worthless masks. She hears the squeak of a wheel. It echoes loudly in the silence. She looks at the door. Her only escape, she moves towards it and exits.

Another corridor, one direction. The naked bulbs overhead this time burning at full brightness. All shadows eliminated with clinical precision. The squeak again. She begins to walk. In the distance ahead she can hear it, the heartbeat, the noise. Her skin clammy. Damp despite the dry air. Footstep after footstep she advances. An abandoned trolley catches her attention. She pauses to look at the rig set up neatly on it, the syringe resting in the stainless steel kidney dish, its needle propped up on the rim, ready to use. Her heart skips a beat, a hidden need eating away through her. She picks up, looks, injects. There had been a choice, and she made it.

Flicker. Above her the lights flicker. Flicker and sway. The shadows returning as the bulbs dim to a dull orange, crawling out of their slumber. The noise rising in volume. She swallows and steps backwards. The smoothness of the wall solid behind her back. She turns, no way back, no escaping to where she had been. The only way forward.

Squeak, drag. Squeak, drag. The sound of a trolley being

pushed. She walks towards it, allowing the shadows to engulf her as she moves with her back against the wall. In the distance she sees the back of a man disappear through a set of double doors. They swing shut behind him like a hospital. She follows. Slipping through the crack and into Hell.

They stand there, pulling the bodies off the trolleys and straight into the furnaces. Three open ovens filled to the brim with the dead. They explode into flames for a second before crumbling to ash and rising up through the chimney to be bellowed out into the world. Body after body consumed with fire. The smell burns her nose like church incense. No scent of burning bodies here, only that of dead religions. Shadows worshiping at their altars of death.

One of the guards turns, he looks at her with dead eyes. 'Name?' he barks. Her voice catches in her throat. He repeats his question, 'Name?'

'What are you doing?' she asks back. Her emotions empty; her head spinning from the scent around her.

'You do not question us. Name?'

'They're, they're—'

'They are parasites, leeches.'

'They're human.'

'They are parasites.'

Rose looks again at the trolley. Large black beetles and worms cover the surface, writhing sickly amongst each other. Another set are plucked and thrown to burn.

'Name?'

Another guard turns and looks. He licks his lipless mouth with his tongue, and smiles grotesquely at her. 'She's the one.' He jumps on the spot. 'She's *the* one.'

Rose takes the cue and runs back through the door and

onto another corridor. Behind her the soldiers follow. Their boots heavy. Backlit she sees their shadows in front of her. They mutate, their bodies hunch, arms turn to legs. Faces elongate. Their number doubles. A pack of jackals chasing. Catching up. She feels their breath against her. One swipes, knocks her off balance and she stumbles.

She hits the ground on all fours and feels her pursuer mount her. Gripping at her waist, biting her neck. It enters without care. Thrusting inside with feral madness. The rest of the pack howl with pleasure. It cums, crumbles to dust against her and the next takes its position. Thrust, thrust, thrust. Crumble. Dust. Another, then another. Then nothing. Spent she falls forward. Tears. Pain. Her womb burning like acid. She feels the oil dribble out of her, expelled by gravity. The pain increases, she doubles up and rolls onto her back.

Alone she pushes, screams. Pushes, pushes. A head emerges from her. Its small dead eyes look at her with lust. It cries out, she pushes once more. Shoulders, arms follow. Its hands grip her thighs and it pulls itself out. The baby looks at her, covered in blood and semen. She crawls backwards away from it, its glare. Away from its impossible erection. Her back meets the wall. No escape. The creature from her womb advances slowly. The shadows growing on each side.

'No,' she pleads. 'Dear God, no.'

The baby's head cocks. Its left arm mutates into a giant syringe, filled with brown liquid, little faces peer at her through the glass.

Rose screams. 'It's just a dream! This is just a fucking dream!'

The needle is pushed into her arm and its contents released. Her muscles relax. Euphoria. Pleasure ejaculating through her body. The purest hit. The purest ecstasy.

Her child enters her, the needle still emptying into her vein. With a warbled gasp it cums deep inside her, at the same moment she orgasms. Without withdrawing, the newborn rots to nothing. The shadows claim the remains of the scene.

*Reality.*

Rose gasps for air. Deep intakes of oxygen. Hyperventilating. Jolted awake she sits up, blinking her eyes to adjust to the gloom. The clock's digital display glows red. 02:30. She focuses on it. Silently it counts away the minutes. Her breathing calms. *Just a dream*, she thinks, although nightmare would have been a better word to use. *Nothing but a dream.*

She looks around for a rig. *So much for cutting down.* She thinks about how much she has used in the past few days since she last spoke to Niente. He had tried to call her, constantly; she had turned her phone off as a response. She had left him crying outside her flat's front door when she refused to open it. It cuts the pain when the needle tears through her skin, but what to make of all the visions, the dreams? Was it not these tears in reality that she was trying to escape? This feeling of change. The staleness in the air she had detected, they had all detected but they had all neglected. The oncoming storm.

*Sod this.* She crawls from the bed. *Dreams can't hurt me. I'm not crazy, it's just Niente rubbing off on me.* One more day, then she will stop. That is the promise she makes to herself. *One more day.*

She lets her feet guide her. Autopilot. A path trodden enough times that thinking is not a necessity. Open door. Hallway. Living room. Stop.

The television flickers. Static rainfall on a dead channel behind a shattered screen. Niente's words flicker through her head. 'When was the last time there was something decent on TV?' She reaches for the remote. Channel 1. Dead. Channel 2. Dead. Channels 3 to 6. Dead. Just clouds of noise hissing out into her flat. One channel left. Her finger hits the button. The channel changes. The remote drops from her hand. Channel 7. Her stunned face looks back at her from the screen. Her room condensed down and locked within the digital box.

She watches her image stumble back, feels her physical form do exactly the same. She sees the shadow emerge from the hallway before she feels its phantom hands grip her shoulders and spin her round. A face forms on the head of the shadow. Hollow sockets for eyes and lips held back by chains. It screams. Dead breath hitting her face. Stale. Bitter. It throws her backwards and continues to form. Red raw skin, bleeding from sour sores, flecks of puss tinting the blood. Long metal blades erupt through its shoulders, rusted nails for fingers.

Rose rubs her eyes viciously. Trying to erase a dream from reality. The figure does not vanish, does not fade like a memory. It jumps for her, its multi-mouthed erection's teeth chattering with excitement, anticipation. She rolls and the creature lands beside her. Without a breath or pause she jumps to her feet and runs. Screaming, the silence engulfs the sound and a whisper is all that is heard. She reaches the front door but finds it locked. *Shit.* What had she expected? Turning she runs to the only safe place. Her bedroom. She slams the door behind her, pulls a drawer in front of it. Nothing chased after her. The flat sleeps in silence. *Hallucination.* She breathes. *Nothing but a hallucination.*

The smell of cigarette smoke. *Shit.*

'Hello.' The voice comes from behind her, from the bed. 'Quite an adventure you are having tonight, my dear, is it not?'

Rose turns. The woman is sat on her bed, her face wrinkled with age. Cigarette one hand, glass of vodka in the other. She smiles smugly at Rose.

'What do you want?' Rose whimpers.

'You know what we want.'

'But I can't.'

'You have already begun.'

'No, this small hurt is for his own good.'

The woman shakes her head. 'And his pain will benefit us all.' A sip. 'Everyone.'

'I don't understand.'

'You are not meant to. That is not your role and already in your mind you secretly know too much.'

'I'm dreaming. You're not real.'

'No?'

'No, this is impossible. I'm not giving in to the demands of some drug induced dream.'

'Fine. If it is persuasion you need.' The woman claps her hand. The room darkens. Rose feels a hand grab her leg, then another. Behind her the darkness edges under the door, a puddle of nothing growing. It begins to take shape. The creature from the living room rising. She can feel it approach. Feel the clothes being ripped from her body. Feel the heat from its penis.

'No,' she cries, trying to find the soul beneath the old woman's eyes. 'Please God, no.'

Pushed forward into a bend. Breath against her neck. One

nailed hand digs into her shoulder, the other her hip. With a gasp she feels the creature enter.

The old woman gets to her feet and advances. She leans into Rose's face and exhales smoke into it. 'We are not "just" a dream.'

# CHAPTER NINE

The phone call had been blunt. Niente did not know what to make of it at first but after sitting on the bench for over an hour it finally sunk in. Rose had told him to 'fuck off.' Fuck off for good. No desire to continue any form of contact. Ever. It cut. It hurt. He had cried openly and without care. At this early hour who was there to matter?

He had started the evening sat outside her front door crying, pleading to no response other than the sound of a key turning in the lock. He had curled up and slept in the open at the bottom of the staircase outside her flat, wearing only his t-shirt and jeans. He remained there until a neighbour shooed him away like a tramp. Following that, he had walked to Milner Square Park and whittled away the hours in silent contemplation. That was when the phone call had been received. Her voice had been flat, broken. Dead. Something sounded lost, a part of her gone, vanished, would never return. He had held the phone to his ear for twenty minutes after she hung up.

Confused he looks out into the dark morning. He is cold, freezing. He should go home and rest but he does not want to be alone. Not there anyway. He looks at his watch. 8:00am. Early still. A whole day ahead of him. *Shit*. He pats down the pockets of his jeans. Clean. Empty. All used up and a morning of normality before he gets home. *No, not home. Anywhere but there. But where?* He knows exactly where.

He gets to his feet and walks away. The girl dressed in black watches him leave. She raises a cigarette to her lips and smiles.

'The usual please.'

The barista stares blankly at him. 'That is?'

'Surely you remember?' Niente laughs. 'I'm not that hard to forget. I'm in here everyday almost.'

'How many people do you think I serve?'

Niente frowns, she genuinely does not recognise him. 'Chai Latte. Cinnamon sprinkled on top.'

'Would you like anything else? A sandwich or cake.'

'Did I ask for anything?'

'Just doing my job,' she replies tartly.

*Autopilot more like.* Niente watches her go about making his drink, places the exact change in her hand when demanded and walks over to One. Sat at the same table, at the same time, with the same coffee to wake himself up after his nightshift. *She doesn't even know his order either,* Niente thinks as he sits on the opposite chair.

'You look like shit,' One says.

'Thanks, nice to see you too.'

'You do, what the fuck have you been doing? At least I've got a reason to look so tired.'

*Here we go.* 'Don't start the job lecture. I'm not in the mood.'

'When are you ever?'

'When did you stop living?'

'When I realized my responsibilities.'

Niente pulls a face and mimics One's response. 'When I

realized my responsibilities and decided to be an upstanding member of society.' Pause. 'How noble.'

'Grow up.'

'One day I might. Just not now.' Niente lifts the cup to his lips and sips at its lukewarm contents.

They glare at each other in silence. Each drinking slowly. One is the first to speak. 'So…' He breaks off.

'So?'

'So why did you want to speak to me? I assume that's why you turned up.'

'I'm worried.' Niente pauses. 'About Rose.'

'No surprise there. What's she done this time? Who's she fucked that she shouldn't?'

'What's with the attitude?'

'I'm just tired. Job, remember?'

'Don't start again.' Niente's voice cracks on the last word, his eyes darting to stare away at an unspecified spot on the ceiling. He clenches his fists against the table top.

'Shit, what's she done?'

'Ended it. Walked away.'

'From you?'

'Yeah.'

'Crap. Why?'

'She's changing. Said she wants to quit.'

'That's good though. You can't blame her if you're not doing it with her.'

'She's not stopped.'

'Oh.'

'She's using more.'

'Ah.'

'I saw her, and spoke to our dealer. She's going crazy.

Something happened last night, I tried calling her but she ignored then called back later. She sounded dead.'

'What are you going to do about it?'

'What can I do? She won't speak to me.'

'Make her. She can't ignore you forever.'

Niente sighs. He knows One makes sense but how do you talk to someone who does not want to be spoken to? How do you get someone back into your life when they do not want to be part of it? How do you fill that void, that rejection?

One's arm stretches across the table and touches Niente's hand. 'You need to. If not for her, for your peace of mind.'

'But she doesn't want me. Without her what have I got?'

'You've got me. You've always had me.'

'You don't understand me, what I feel. She does.'

'I try to.'

'Sometimes "try" isn't enough.'

One sighs. 'Go speak to her. Wait for her to leave and catch her on the street. She can't ignore you for long.'

'What, stalk her? I'm sure she'll love that.'

'It'll show you care. It's got to be better than being here drinking coffee and worrying.' He reaches into his wallet and pulls out a note. 'Here, go get yourself sorted and then sort all this crap out. You two need each other.'

'What?' Niente takes the money as One nods. 'Erm, thanks.'

Needle. Vein. Push. Euphoria. Niente slumps back onto the sofa, his eyes glaze over and reflect the static from the television's dead channel. His hand on the remote, he does not change it. What would be the point?

The static bleeds out from the screen, filling the room like a snowstorm. Wrapping its digital arms around him. Swirling, distorting until that is all he can see. Black rain and white snow. The snow blackens until there is only the darkness. The darkness and the noise. The noise he has grown so used to hearing. Twisted, dirty. Rising and falling like the mumble of the dead.

*There.*

The sky is white, featureless. The ebony snow falls from a hidden infinity, falling straight to the earth. A blanket of black in a world of white. A girl sits by the tree. Her glass legs crossed. She smiles at him. Beckons him over.

'So,' she says. 'What have you learned? All those questions now running through your head.' She stands. 'Any conclusions?'

'No,' Niente answers.

'Oh dear. That stupid? It will become clear in time. Your determination for answers has been numbed. I guess for that girl.' She smirks. 'Rose is her name is it not?'

'What have you done to her? If you've touched her I'll…'

'You will what? Touch me?' Her face distorts, the skin peeling and ageing. 'Would you touch me now?' She licks her lips and grips Niente's groin with her cold hand. He tries to pull away but he cannot. Frozen on the spot. 'Here you are mine. And to answer your question, *I* have not touched her.'

'Good.'

'That is not to say others have not.' Her fingers unzip his jeans.

Repulsion. 'What the fuck are you doing?' Niente ties to move again but he cannot will his body to do so. Against his will, his cock grows hard and she pulls it out through his fly.

'I do not see you trying to escape. What you need is a shock to snap your mind back to the task I have given you.'

'Stop it.'

'Make me.' She drops to her knees and swallows his cock into her mouth.

*Reality.*

Niente wakes with a start, his breath held in his lungs. He exhales with deep breaths, drawing the air deep into him. *Why do I have a hard-on?* he thinks, as he sees that his cock is out of his pants, standing firm, a drop of pre-cum glistening on its head. He focuses on it and then remembers. Himself inside the hag's mouth. *Why won't that woman just fuck off and leave my dreams alone?* His mind whirls its way through everything the past weeks have forced upon him. How can he make sense of something that does not make sense?

He gets to his feet and puts his cock away; he has no intention of relieving it whilst that image is still in his mind. Walking into his flat's kitchen area, he picks up the collection of newspapers on the table. Their dates the same. Three years ago and nobody has noticed. The same news printed each day. A constant loop. *Are people really that blind?*

Rose. He needs to show her these. Maybe it will snap her back to sense; it is also a reason for him to go see her. He puts everything into a bag. Pulls it over his shoulder. He makes his way into his bedroom and checks him reflection in the full-length mirror. His erection is not too noticeable. *Good.* He leaves the flat, locking the door behind him as he goes.

Niente waits in the shadows outside the steps to her flat. From his position he can see her door without being seen from above. He does not feel comfortable, feels like he is betraying her trust, but he needs to know, needs to see her.

Her door opens and she stumbles out. He wants to cry, she looks almost unrecognisable. Unkempt, dark bags under her eyes and her ginger hair hanging limp and dirty. He follows her onto the street and then he makes his move. 'Rose,' he calls out. She ignores him, so he touches her shoulder and turns her. 'Rose, it's me.'

Her dead eyes look at him, glazed and empty. 'What do you want?' Voice blank, emotionless.

'To check that you are okay.'

'I'm fine. Now you've seen me, can you leave me alone?'

'I'm worried about you. What have I done that's so bad that I deserve this?'

'I told you before.' She makes to leave. 'I'm not telling you again.'

'That's just it, you haven't told me.'

Turning her head back towards him she calmly says, 'It doesn't matter.'

'What's your fucking problem?' Niente snaps.

'You are,' she shouts back. 'Can't you see that you are the fucking problem? You always have been.'

'No, your fucking extreme drug use is. I know that you've been using more than usual. I'm not fucking stupid. I thought you wanted to quit.'

'You know nothing.'

'Then tell me.'

'Look, what do you want? Really? All those fucking messages on my phone. What is so important that you can't give me a bit of peace?'

'Well, look at this.' He pulls out his evidence. 'I've been

getting these each day, freshly printed, freshly delivered.'

'You're collecting newspapers now?' She laughs coldly.

'Look, same date, same content.'

She does not look. 'You've finally cracked, finally lost it.'

'What? You were just as serious as me about the changes we're feeling. Those disturbances. Surely this proves something is happening.'

'That was then.'

'What's changed?'

'Everything.'

'I don't understand.'

'You don't need to. All you need to know is that I want you to leave me alone.'

'Rose? Talk to me.'

She spits in his face. 'You did this to me. *You* did. Now just leave me alone. You should sort yourself out really. I hope you do what's best for you and accept all the help you can get. Just fuck off out of my life.'

Niente lets her push him back, causing him to stumble. He watches her rush away, too numb to answer her back; his throat could not allow him to either, suddenly drying up as his body sends its moisture to other areas. His eyes mirror his brain, misty, unable to process or comprehend what is gong on. Lost and alone. *What's happened to her?*

*Why won't he just go away?* Rose thinks as the machine validates her card, opening the barriers to let her walk through. *I did what they wanted, why won't they all just leave me alone?*

She rushes through Highbury and Islington station, bustling past the other commuters, not stopping to apologize as her shoulders knock them out of her way. She pauses to catch her thoughts on the escalator, using its predictable pace to slow her breathing. She looks forward, ignoring the flames burning above the heads of the select few. Something pulls her attention to the ascending side. She swallows hard. That woman, today in the guise of someone Rose's age, rises towards her, the darkness clouding above her head. The cigarette departs from her lips and she smiles cruelly. Exhaling. She raises her glass of vodka with a nod.

'Fuck off and leave me alone!' Rose screams at her as they pass.

Everyone turns to look at Rose and the empty step rising away from her. With a cry, Rose runs down the rest of the steps. The judgmental whispers washing over her.

On the platform she stands against the wall. *What's happening to me? I did what they asked, why won't they just leave me alone?* She looks at the rotten world around her. Empty inside; her will raped away by the constant nightmares. Never ending shadows groping at her. No escape. Constant pain. Screaming from within, not even the needle takes the noise away anymore. Just a stale prayer to a phantom messiah sat decomposing on his throne, the life exited from him long ago. Those were the visions she saw. The end of everything. The encroaching darkness.

The wind blows against her body, flicking her hair across her face. She straightens up and steps forward. She likes the sound of the Tube train whistling through the tunnel towards the platform. She always has. It reminds her of her childhood. *That seems a long time ago,* she sighs mentally. Lost in the scars upon her arm. She steps closer to the approaching train. Waiting for it to pull up in front of her.

One step.

# CHAPTER TEN

He had seen it with his own eyes. Running onto the platform at the exact moment of impact. He wished it had happened in slow motion but her last moments were split second. A stunned silence then the noise returned. The screaming, the commotion. The shadow standing at the end of the platform.

Back at his flat he had stared into the mirror. His shock paled face speckled with her blood. He had cried. He felt the pressure in his head. His mind wanting to explode. The last thing he remembered was his head hitting the sink basin.

*There.*

Eyes open, awake. *Shit.* He tries to focus. *Where am I?* He checks himself, tapping down all important areas. Keys, wallet, phone. Cock, ass. None have been taken; none have been used. He sits back, relaxes. *Breathe. Focus.*

Rain spits down on him. *Think, what do I do? Look around; find out location.* He looks. He is sat in an alleyway; it is dark, night. It could be anywhere, they all look the same. He pushes his head back against the wall. *Breathe.* His head hurts, so he places a hand against it, it feels wet. Bringing his hand to his face he looks. Red. Lick. Blood. *Oh yeah, sink.*

'You could have done quite a bit of damage if you had not passed out.'

He knows that voice. Without looking, his heart sinks. It is her. 'What do *you* want?'

A cancerous chuckle. 'Is that anyway to greet a friend?' Niente hears her inhale on her cigarette. 'And besides we could not have you damaging yourself too much. Not yet anyway.'

He finally looks at her. As old and wrinkled as the moment they first met. 'What do you want?'

'You know what I want. Did you answer those questions? Did you seek out the truth?'

'All I got was more questions.'

'That is not an answer.' She inhales again. Looks around her and exhales. 'You do choose some dire places do you not?'

'Can't you make sense for once?'

'There is no sense to be made. There are facts and there are fictions. These are all you need to concern yourself with at the moment. It does not matter if they "make sense".'

Niente screams in frustration, launches himself and punches the hag in the face. She recoils back, her teeth exploding out like shards of glass. Her head hits the wall with a crack. Blood sprays everywhere as her head decapitates on its own accord.

He stumbles backwards, the blood clings to the wall like graffiti.

FIND ME IN YOUR WORLD, OR DIE IN MINE.

*Reality.*

The blood had pooled around him; as his eyes flicker open he lifts his head from the sticky red. Looking at the broken mirror he sees a fractured reflection. The cuts on his hand mirror those on the glass. *This is too much,* he thinks. *This is way too much.*

Niente stumbles from the bathroom and walks through to the living room, supporting himself with a hand against the wall. He pauses in the doorway, carefully eyeing up the position of the sofa. With a deep breath he pushes himself forward using the doorframe and staggers towards his goal. Slumped into the chair, he stares at the static flickering on the television screen. His hand on the remote he does not change the channel. Zoned out. Words flicker on the screen like it was a visualizer for his thoughts. *Find me in your world, or die in mine.*

*What does that mean? Shit like this doesn't happen.* It does to the broken. This is life on an eternal high. He scrapes his brain for information. The world has been crumbling for some time. Brick by gradual brick. Neglected, alone. The lost sheep. *Lost sheep need a shepherd to guide them.* Does that make sense? What if he is the shepherd? *What if I'm the shepherd?* He cannot concentrate. His brain filled with tar. How long has there been a tear of the realities? Surely, he would have been aware. They all would have noticed. *It is just the drugs. Just the drugs.*

Something switches in his brain. Switches to the negative and a fuse burns out. He does not feel it. As silent a change over as death. The Passover. His finger twitches, the channel changes. The static remains the same.

*There.*
Eyes open. *As usual.* That is how it always begins. He is in a basketball court; *no, is it a tennis court?* It changes with each degree of a turn. Maybe it is both. At the bottom is a river.

A massive river. It runs smoothly by. Then the ballet begins, gracious dancers gliding along with elegant steps. Children run; play entwining the dancers, splashing in the water of the river.

Dogs run, play. Bark and beg for food. All different breeds, sizes. Healthy coats, tongues lapping up the atmosphere around them.

He turns to the main exit, the tall staircase. As he manoeuvres his way through the masquerade marionettes, a woman steps in the way, her face featureless. A small dog looks up at him from her arms. A Chihuahua with *her* face. Old and haggard. Cigarette held between sharp canines. She spits it out and smiles. 'Now is not the time. Truth can only be found in the dark.'

'Fuck off.'

'Now, now, is that anyway to speak to a lady?'

Niente grabs the dog by its neck and throws it across the vast space of the ballroom. Gasps of shock. Silence. All eyes upon him. Cold stares that tell him he is not welcome. Black snow begins to fall from the ceiling. It settles. He feels the urge to run. He does so. Pushing his way through the frozen mannequins that force themselves towards him. They shatter as they hit the floor. Glorious ejaculations of glass. Woman merges with man; father with daughter. MDMA crystals born from human souls. They crunch under his feet.

Run. Run. Hand on door. Push. Fall.

Cold. The wind is so cold. The sun burns against his naked skin. He is wearing nothing but a bathing towel. Wrapped around his waist. The wind stops. It is a summer's afternoon. He looks around him as he starts to walk.

He is on an amusement promenade. A pier. Stretching out into the sea. The boardwalk empty. Alone. The buildings bright. Painted. The fun echoing off them. He closes his eyes, breathes in. His eyes open. People. Hundreds of people enjoying themselves. Enjoying the day. Families, young lovers. Friends. *Alone. A flash of ginger. Could it be?*

*Focus.* Hair, her hair amongst the crowd. *Rose? Oh please God, let it be her.* He cannot speak. Mute. *Fuck.* She disappears into the moving masses. He pushes forward; forcing himself to walk. Slow movements, his brain frustrated, it feels as though he is walking through tar. *I need to get to her. I need to hold her.* He has lost her once, there is no way he can lose her again. *Why can't I move? Fucking hell, what is wrong with my legs?*

'What are you doing? Standing there like that?'

He spins around. The towel almost falls, but he grabs it before it can. *Who? What? Fuck.* The scene changes and he sees four forms sat on a bench, sticks of candyfloss in their hands. The girl in red, no older than thirteen, the fifteen year-old boy with sticks for legs, a life-sized threadbare teddy. The fourth keeps her face hidden from sight.

'You going to answer?' the voice of the girl.

'Erm, I'm looking for somebody.'

'Who? Oh, we could help. Couldn't we, Boy? It has been so long since we have had such adventure.'

The teddy bear, who Niente assumes is Boy, pats her head mournfully. 'Longer than you think, \*\*\*\*.'

The name gets censored. A high-pitched din eradicates the identity. Niente shakes his head clean of it. Reality. No, *is it?*

*Fuck.*

Who knows anymore?

'Don't you think so, Arthur?'

*What?* Blink. He has missed part of the conversation. 'What was that?'

'Hmm?'

'You said something didn't you?'

'Did I?' the girl.

'Yes.'

'Did she?' Boy.

'Yes!'

'I do believe…' Arthur.

'What?'

'Hmm?' All three.

'Fuck off,' Niente screams. *What the fuck is this?*

The sea whispers in his ear. A name. One name. Rose. Rose.

*Rose!*

*That's what I'm meant to be doing.* 'I can't take this anymore.' He makes to leave.

'Don't leave us,' the girl.

'Please don't leave poor [CENSORED] alone again,' the boy, Arthur.

*Don't listen to them. Close ears.*

A whisper filters through. 'Don't leave.'

'Don't leave.'

'Don't leave.'

'Leave.'

He snaps back to reality. *Reality?* No, he has already had that thought. A hand on his wrist. Gripping tight. Old, jaundiced, frail. He allows his eyes to track her features back through the bruises and heroin scars that pepper up her arm. He reaches the face. Sunken, featureless, grey. Our rotten future staring back at him. Her mouth grinds together. Teeth on teeth. It sets a tick off in Niente's eye. Her grip relaxes and he reaches to pull the white hair from her face. A black tear rolls down her cheek.

'Who are you?'

'Run. Leave. This is not the place.'

'What?'

'Don't die in this world. Please don't. Save yourself. Run.' She climbs to her feet. 'Run.' Her legs buckle under her. Her head explodes as it hits the floor. A bracelet remains, shining on top of the ashes. He reaches for it. Lifts it. Examines. Breathes. He knows the bracelet, knows its owner. It was Rose's prize possession. She went nowhere without wearing it. *Rose?* He looks down at the desiccated remains at his feet. 'Rose?'

'Run,' a voice says from inside his head. 'Run!'

He runs.

There is nowhere left to run. The pier cut off from the mainland. Shattered skeletal beams poke out, revealed by the gaps in the rotten wood. Niente stands looking out to sea. *What the fuck am I meant to do now? Where am I meant to go?* No way forward, only back. But maybe that is the truth of the matter. You can only go forward if you look back. The future lies in the past; the present just frames it.

The sea is turbulent, its black waves slap against the pier. There is a storm coming. A drop of rain hits his hand. It runs away like ink. Black rain. The wind picks up and lashes his towel away. Naked he stands. He outstretches his arms and screams. The sky rips open and pisses its regrets down upon him. Us. Everyone is screaming into *la mer*. They scream. The rain consumes our skin. They fade. He fades. *Ne priez pas pour mon âme, elle est deja morte.*

*Reality.*
His eyes open with his sharp intake of air. Awake. An alarm is ringing somewhere in the flat. A constant monotone staccato pattern. He tries to stand, he cannot. He is not really awake. The alarm fades, the needle falls from between his fingers. He does not even realize he had done it.

*There.*
The ballroom. Night. *How did I get back here? Maybe I didn't leave.* In the moonlight the place looks decrepit, worn out. Tired. Paint peeling under the pale blue beam. Dust swirling like mist.

Niente hears something move, the slow motion of movement wading through shallow water. *The river.* He moves towards it. A rocky bank and a pathetic stream all that is left. The dog at its heart looks at him. A Golden Retriever. Its fur sodden, dirty. It begins to advance, cautiously sniffing the air as it limps, dragging a useless leg behind it. A pathetic wag of the tail. A tongue hangs from its rotten mouth, its face half skeleton.

'What's happened to you?' Niente asks, his voice soft, sad.

'We all have to try and survive. We hide in the shadows, we shun the light. This is our domain. This is what happens when you live in silence. This is what you all will become.'

Niente steps back in unison with the dog's front paw. It

is not going to let the gap between them widen. 'What? Why can't anyone give me an easy answer?'

'We are the forgotten, the abandoned and unborn. We are the un-thought hopes and the unrealised dreams. We are the quiet. The silence. The faded homes of forgotten memories. Our keys long since misplaced and broken. We are the broken. We all rot down here. We were allowed in. Your kind were spat into the void.'

'What?' Niente falls back over a chair. The noise is creates rumbles like thunder.

'You came here, now we feed. The lost soul.' It sniffs the air in front of it. 'No, you are not lost. You too are abandoned.' It stops. Looks beyond Niente's form. 'It's okay. We can't touch him.'

Niente hears a shadow move behind him. It forms another Golden Retriever. Female, her unborn pup hanging half birthed from her vagina. Sat next to her partner she licks its head lovingly. 'He's the one?' she whispers.

The male nods. 'He's the abandoned. The broken. He is the one who will never be fixed.'

It turns away from Niente and is followed by his partner. Their forms merge, melt together. A tall shadow rising up. Tall, gaunt. Tendrils of smoke surrounding it. He should have noticed from the way the dogs spoke. *Darkness, my old friend.* The shadow continues to move away.

'Wait! Why are you abandoning me now? Why here when I need you the most. Or was this the moment you once spoke of?'

The shadow doesn't turn.

'Answer me! Goddamn it, answer me!'

Silence.

A blink of an eye and the scene changes. The boardwalk. Traders are packing away their belongings, their day of trade over. Money made and now they can sleep quietly at night. Niente walks; he is naked. In the crowd before him he can see a red flame burning, moving away from him. *Follow the red flame.* Rose was a red flame. He follows. Follows. Everyone else's existence is nothing but a blur at the corner of his vision, the only thing in focus is the flame. *Follow the flame.*

*No, this isn't right.* Back at the ruined end of the pier. *What?* He knows this is a dead-end, so he stops and wonders why he bothered coming this far. *Let her go.* One final kiss blown out to sea.

*So, back here it seems. Butting my head against a brick wall. What if I was to jump into the sea? That would work right? Who knows what to do anymore? Just jump and bring all the noise to an end.* A peaceful end. The sad happy ending. The broken-hearted Hollywood ending.

*Fuck that! That's far too easy. What would it solve? What would happen to the unanswered questions? What would I learn? Peaceful death or unknown future? Surely the shit makes the picture look homely.*

He turns and walks back towards the funfair. Deep in thought, he almost bumps straight into him. 'One?'

'Niente?' One looks equally as shocked.

'What are you doing here?'

'Looking.'

'Looking for what?'

'I don't know. I've forgotten.'

They continue their journey together, barely speaking. One's company more than adequate to calm, stabilize and make Niente feel protected. Happy. A hint of a smile on his lips.

One is suddenly pulled away from Niente. A dirty old fortune-teller grips One's arm with his tanned fingers. 'You. I read you free,' his wizened face says. 'I see your future. I see your soul.'

One tries to pull away. 'I don't want to know.'

'But you must.' The fortune-teller smiles, showing two rows of rotten teeth. 'Il free so don't worry.'

One shrugs and looks at Niente. 'It's free, I guess.' He is led out of sight.

Alone again, Niente sees a doorway. The shadow stands next to it. Tall, gaunt. He waves; the shadow stays stationary and gives nothing in return. At the door he tries the handle. It opens. The shadow screams, explodes. Thousands of flies wrap themselves against Niente's naked form. Forcing their way into his throat, nose. He cannot breathe. He is drowning. He is drowning.

*Reality.*

One jolts awake. The dream had been too real. Too clustered. He had found what he had been looking for. He rubs his eyes, and Niente was in his dream. Could they really have been dreaming it in unison? Were they looking for the same thing? Albeit for different reasons.

He reaches for his clock and checks the time. 07:30. *Too early to give Niente a call?* He looks at his phone. *Maybe.* On his feet he stumbles to the bathroom. The water is warm against his face. He looks at his reflection. He needs to shave. Razor in hand; ready for the first stroke. *Fuck it. You know what? Fuck it.* He places the razor back on its stand. Something changes.

Destiny rewritten.

*That sums it up.* He pauses his thoughts. *That makes no sense.* Press play and he carries on. He returns to the bedroom. Why did Niente have to show him those newspapers? Surely there is some error somewhere. Maybe Niente is just wrong. Maybe he had never been wrong. *Too many maybes. Far too many maybes.*

Sat on the bed, head in hands, One tries to recall the fundamentals of his previous dreams and conversations. Everything has pointed to change, its presence thick in the air. He has felt this way for sometime, getting stronger every day, every morning. Every second. What could it all mean?

His hand reaches for the phone.

He dials the number.

It rings through.


Niente's eyes snap open. Awake. He jumps to his feet. Lightheaded. All sensory vision blurs. Images. Faces and conversations blinking to life, then dying silently as quickly as they had begun. *Think. Focus.* Vision clears, and he finds himself on the floor. *Try to focus.* Blurred vision. He shakes his head. *Slowly refocus.* Still on the floor. *Must have blacked out,* he thinks as he once again rises to his feet.

Think, ignore the tar mind and filter through it. He searches. Searches for answers, explanations, reasons. He searches blind. Nothing steps forward. A black shroud over everything. The remnants of a wasted dream. What had he learnt? What was he *meant* to have learnt? He rubs his hand down his face. *Why the fuck is this happening? Why now?* He tries to scream. It dies in his throat. His vision blurs again and he sways on the spot. Dizzy. He crouches down. Head in his hands. *Breathe*. In. Out. *Count to five*. One. Two. Three. Four. Five. *Breathe*. Slowly. In. Out. In. Out. Sigh.

*I must look like a right state*. He forces a grin. *What the fuck must I look like?*

*Stand up*. Unsteady on his feet he turns off the television. In the kitchen he makes himself a coffee. Strong, double the amount of his normal sugar. *Calm. Calm*. He takes a sip. He needs a cigarette. A model's diet: coffee and a cigarette. He returns to the living room.

The television bleeds static. He frowns at the screen, sure that he had turned it off. The static falls eternally constant, it makes no sound. A vision of infinity. He picks up the remote and presses the 'off' button. The screen pinpoints with a click. He listens to the sound of his existence, the muffled noises from outside filter through. Life. Life disconnected from his. Dissociation. He closes his eyes as images of Rose flash across his mind, bleeding in from his subconscious, forcing him to remember how much he misses Rose. How incomplete he feels in her absence. A piece missing and for what? This world is not what it seems. He needs to find the answers for himself. He needs to understand. It feels like his destiny to do so.

*Fuck*. He bends to his knees and snorts from the table.

*This is my life. This is my existence*. The rolled £10 note he drops from his fingers says it all. This is existence; this is him living a life. *What a wasted life*, he ponders. *Wasted but simple. Everything sorted through a line, a small grainy existence that dissociates everything. This line means more than that. This is the truth. The way. The way in which all my dreams turn to…* He stops. *Wait. This isn't the point where everything all turns to gold. There is no gold. This is the line. This is the line that will lead me to the truth.* 'Truth' he says aloud. 'What is true?'

Pause.

The ketamine block ends and he continues to think. *Okay, so this is 'reality'? I get it.* He does not get it but he convinces himself that everything is all right. *There is no reality, there is no... no... there is nothing.*

*What?*

He looks, tries to focus again. *Oh my god,* he thinks. *I'm such a fuck up.*

Staggering to the bathroom he splashes cold water onto his face. Breathes. In. Out. *What the fuck is happening?* The mirror reflects his cracked image back at him. His eyes look clouded. Open. A new depth to them he had not noticed before. They seem darker, clearer. Opposite upon opposite.

Blink.

*What the fuck?*

Another splash of water. *Am I really this wasted?* Deep breath. Nothing is making any sense. Nothing. Nothing.

Nothing.

Nothing.

Nothing.

His hands grip the sink basin. *Focus. Why can't I fucking focus?*

He focuses. Blue eye meets blue eye. It is not a true reflection; it is what he perceives to be the truth. *That's it!* 'That's it!'

The phone rings, it vibrates in his pocket. He pulls it out and places it to his ear. 'We can only see a perception of the truth,' he mumbles into it.

'What?' One.

'We can only see a perception of the truth.'

'No, I heard you, but what?'

'Humour me. Go with it. We can only know what is told to us, what we are led to believe.'

'Okay.'

'So if someone tells us a lie but we see that as truth, what does that make the lie?'

'A lie.'

'In your perspective.'

'What? Niente, a lie is a lie.'

'Not if it's a truth.'

'You're wasted.'

'No, I'm thinking.'

'What?'

'Truth is something we *believe* to be real.'

'No, truth is something that *is* real.'

'Not if it was a lie to begin with.'

'Niente, seriously, what are you on?'

'I've cracked it One. I know what that bitch has been aiming for me to learn.'

'What?'

'Everything is a perspective. We believe it true so we can function as normal and according to plan.'

'Niente.' One's voice is sharp, concerned. 'What the fuck have you taken?'

'A lot, but now I understand.'

'Understand?'

'Yeah, sheep do as they are told. The shepherd manipulates them. *This*, everything is a manipulation of some kind. I'm broken. I can see the cracks that the blind can't see and the lost gloss over. It's rotting, falling apart and only the broken can see it. Everyone else is an armchair observer.'

'Niente, we need to talk.'

'We are talking.'

'Get dressed, meet me at our usual place.'

'As structured.'

'No as *usual*.'

'Habit.'

'You don't need to tell me about that word.'

Niente walks into the Costa next to Mornington Crescent station. As the door closes behind him, he wishes One would meet him at Starbucks instead more often, but this his usual place. The usual time. He knows how the scene is going to pan out. One will be sat at the same table, drinking the same coffee. The waitress will say the same script even though she should know by now.

'Chai latte.'

'What…' The recording begins again.

'Just a chai latte. Cinnamon sprinkles on top. No sandwich, no cake. Just a simple chai latte.'

'Okay.' She smiles her fake smile and makes the coffee.

'Okay, just go about your job. No questions, no memory. You're a fucking drone. Stupid fucking drone.' He leans over the counter and pushes his face up to hers. 'A stupid fucking drone.'

Static burst.

He is stood waiting by the counter. The waitress hands him his chai latte. 'Anything else with that sir?'

*What the fuck?*

'No, that's fine.' He pays and goes to sit opposite his friend. As expected, there is a momentary silence. 'So…'

'How you holding up?' One looks Niente in the face.

'Shit.'

'Oh.'

'What'd you expect? Me dancing around the streets?'

'Don't need to be like that. I understand.'

'Do you?' Niente snaps. He breathes deeply. 'Sorry.'

'Let me look at that cut, yeah?'

Niente glares. Pause. A few sips. Silence. 'So…' Niente's hands fidget, each rubbing their thumb against the index finger. Uncomfortable, he does not know why. This is his oldest friend yet they have nothing to say on a personal level. Their minds spinning out questions and ideas but unable to word them. 'You said you wanted to talk.'

'Yeah, I do.'

'This isn't going to be another lecture is it? Yaddy yadda. I know I'm taking too much but it's helping.'

'It's not about that, that's the last thing on my mind.' One watches as Niente casts an unfocused eye around the café. His lower jaw slack. *He looks like such a mess,* One thinks. *You can see his addiction on him.* 'Did you have a weird dream last night?'

'I always have weird dreams.' Niente laughs.

'You dreamt of a pier, a fortune-teller and a red flame.'

Niente's face drops. 'How'd you know?' Sobriety rushes over his figure. 'How the hell did you know?'

'I dreamt the same dream.'

'What?'

'You were in my dream. I know I was in yours. Close enough to touch physically. I know if I tell you word for word what happened you would already know. Our dream states crossed a fate path in reality. We entwined for that one moment. Connected direct. Didn't you find that weird? It felt so real.'

'This isn't the first time is it?'

'What?'

'All those times you sat there and bitched at me for doing drugs, that everything was all their fault, but you knew. You knew that something was coming.'

One makes eye contact. 'I know. I'm sorry. I had to. It was too much for me to think about it. I have responsibilities you know. I did it because I cared, but now, now Rose has gone, they happen more. Disturbed my routine. I didn't shave today. I shave *every day*; always have, but the dream changed that. One small thing and now everything is different. I don't like it. It doesn't feel real.'

'Reality is only a perception of the truth.'

'What?'

'That's what that dream did for me. I learnt nothing within that world, only when I woke. But I don't know what's what. That's exactly what I wanted to talk to you about.'

They click. The one thing they could not word was the one thing they wanted to. Connected. Connection. True connection. It feels real. A lost memory bleeds in and multiples its impact by millions. Reality.

One breaks the stare and raises lukewarm coffee to his lips. The café life just flashes past them at the speed of light. Morning, day, night. Morning, day, night. Days, years. Time stopped. Irrelevant. Locked in the moment. He returns the cup to the table. Thud. Everything returns to normal. No one has aged. No one has left. The coffee remains lukewarm. 'So what are we gonna do about it?'

'What can we do about it? It's not like we can do anything.' Niente looks nervously around him.

'Yes, yes we can.'

'You seem more positive than usual.'

'So?'

'What if we're seeing totally different things? How do you know what's what?'

'We look at the facts. Something's changed and I want to understand why. I know you're probably more messed up than me but—'

'Thanks.' Niente smirks as he sits back into his seat.

'Well, you know what I mean. You keep saying you felt the need to find something out. You said you'd worked it out, and you've got those newspapers, right?'

'Yeah, but it's, you know, weird. Like I solved one riddle to be faced with another that can't be answered without the first. A self-fulfilling prophecy. I don't know if I want to understand anymore.'

'Niente, you have to. You're the only one who can do it. Remember you always believed you'd have that "moment". *The* moment. This is it. I feel it. You need to understand otherwise you won't be able to move forward. You'll just fester. Break the chain. Do what you have always done. Go against the system.'

Niente giggles to himself at a memory. 'That's revolutionary.'

One smiles. 'Want to break something?'

'Always.'

# CHAPTER ELEVEN

Niente returned to the Underground after his chat with One, who had left for work. Alone, he sits disconnected as the train rattles along the lines. He rubs his nose, letting his high kick in. The train stops and its doors open. People get on. The train leaves the station.

He looks up; he goes cold. Sitting directly opposite is *him*. The guy he had met when he had been with Rose. His eyes stare right into Niente's soul. He cannot break eye contact. They sit in silence, their minds trying to connect. Failure. The guy smiles at Niente, his mouth opens, the train slows. Niente stumbles out of the exit and onto the platform. *What the fuck is going on?* he thinks. Scratching at the elements within his mind. So hard to focus in a reality created from a reality. He can't tell where the ends meet. When does one become the other? *This is reality, right? Even if it is colorized by all the drugs.* A twinge in his temple. A pain. He rubs it and tries to ease its pulse.

Reality is just a perspective of the truth.

Reality is what is *real*. So, can all this truly be happening? The world crumbling around him and there is no definition. How long has he been disconnected from all this? Protected in a bubble. Now he needs to break out. Or will that just be another paranoid trip into his mind? He rubs his eyes. The brain pressure clears and eyes focus. If only he could see the auras Rose had seen. Pinpoint all the key players and question them for answers. Why are there never any answers?

He composes himself and walks along the platform. It seems longer than normal. Stretching into the horizon. He lets his eyes open fully. He sees it all. The shadows standing next to each person, alive, like smoke, biding their time. Following like guardians. Their empty eyes bleeding out grey trails. Connected to the host but still unborn. They wait. The second hand ticks towards their hour. *How patient.*

The walls peel away, decay and rot. Brown trails of slime run through broken cracks. The people flicker like projections. Digital representations of life. As sterile as television. They move as planned, as structured. The sun rises, falls; they do the same. Marching forward to the sound of someone else's drum. Sheep. Lost sheep. His eye twitches; their faces change. All determination and drive filters away to grey. Drones on autopilot, waiting for the next update and creation of need. Waiting. Waiting.

Waiting. Everyone seems to be waiting. Waiting for what? A train? A job? A message? God? That is all we seem to do. Wait. Wait in line, wait your turn. Wait to speak. Wait to act.

*Argh!* He claws at his face and sits on a bench. He has only walked a few paces. *What the hell is wrong with me?*

*Find me in your world, or die in mine.*

He shakes his head. *I will find you, and you will tell me what's going on.* One was right, they need answers. Everyone needs answers. Niente will not wait in line until his number is called. He takes a deep breath. No panic. No overdose. Everything will work; he just needs a moment to gather his thoughts. One, two, three, four. *Right. Move.* Even if everyone knows he is wasted, what does it matter? All he wants to do is to leave the rat holes and face the sky. Step, step. Stay behind the yellow line.

The girl falls down the escalator. A bone breaks on every step, her face rips and sprays ribbons of blood into the air in spirals. She is dead before she reaches the bottom. Nobody stops to help her; nobody watches her fall. She died years ago. This is her memory. The Sunday repeat. Her body in a bundle on the ground and everyone just walks by, stepping over the invisible corpse. The blood pools around her.

Niente looks up at the escalator as he steps on. He rises. *Please stand on the right.* The girl trips, she falls from the top and rolls straight past him. Her blood whispers against his body. Someone just pressed replay. He follows her descent from his rising angle. Her body twists, snaps. Breaks. From so high she looks like a doll. Caught in a cycle. Niente watches her final twitch as he is pushed forward by the people behind him. Always moving towards something. The rush. Push. Push. Always got to be the first one there. *That's probably how she died,* he laments. *A small mouse in the path of a tiger.*

Mankind on its march forward. Forward to what? There is a great big nothing. The future is a hollow word. A void. An infinite. We walk forward towards the sun but does it get any closer? Niente falls to the floor, his back against the wall. *Fuck, what a sight.* He watches the forest of legs. *What are we moving for? Where are any of us going?*

*Stop. Think. Okay.* His eyes focus. *Kinda.* They spiral into another reality. Reality merges with the dream state. *No. Focus.* Stop. Breathe.

'Are you okay?' A female voice.

'I'm fine.' Niente smiles at her. She is mid-thirties, almost motherly. She should be caring for a baby, not a man. 'I just felt a bit faint.' His eyes drop away from the stranger and focus on his hands, pale and shaking, clammy. His face feels the same, damp, drained, sickly.

'Oh, are you sure?' Reassuring hand on the knee. Her concern is causing others to stop. 'Should I call for a supervisor or a doctor?'

Niente laughs. 'No, no. I'm good. You know, just been busy. Overworked. Haven't eaten properly.'

'It's too early to be busy. It's okay.' She looks him over. 'I understand.' She nods to the others who have grouped around. They leave. 'Now, you'll be okay. Just breathe, okay?'

'Thank you.'

'Skipped breakfast didn't you?'

'Yes.' He is instigating conversation. *Why?* He does not know. It helps him. He tries to stand. Unsteady. He feels what little colour had remained in his face drain away. 'I'll be okay.' He smiles. The druggy smile. 'Thank you.'

'I'll help you walk a few paces then we'll see how you go.'

'Okay.' Stumble, shuffle, stumble. 'Thank you.'

Niente's hand touches the wall, he wishes he could crawl into it but he knows he must keep his composure. He looks into the stranger's face. She looks at his eyes without judgment and rubs his back.

'I'll be fine from here, thank you,' Niente says, his voice weak.

'Are you sure?'

'Yeah, totally.'

'Okay.' The woman begins to pull away. 'Take care of yourself.' She melts, and joins the rest of the population and disappears from sight. The Good Samaritan. One small hope

for his vision of mankind. Selfless, un-judgmental help from a stranger. Her life crossed his and they will never see each other again. This moment locked in three places. Her mind, his mind and the surroundings.
A little girl runs past him towards the escalator. He smiles.

Outside the fresh air wakes him up. He runs across the street to the shop and buys some cigarettes. *Endlessly seeking meaning.* He pushes the pack into his back pocket and smirks as he leaves. *Brain, why do you always need to think like that?*
He is happy. For some reason that small moment has made him smile. A positive in all the pieces of shit that have been following him lately. He kicks an imaginary piece of dirt on the floor and walks back towards his flat.

Melted to his sofa. This is how he is. This is life. His life. He sits and pulls a cigarette from the pack. Click, flame, inhale. He feels selfish. Broken. He cannot squeeze another tear out for Rose. She has gone. There is no coming back. She has no future to call her own. Life just rolls on. One frequency deleted and pulled from existence. The Earth feels every death, every creation. But what makes his existence any different? *What makes any of this different?* Nothing. Belief. Truth. This moment. *The* moment. He stubs his cigarette out in the ashtray. The song ends. He smiles. How like life. Birth the initial flame, conception the spark, then the inhalation and exhalation. Breathe in; breathe out all the shit. Live like a cigarette burning bright. The cherry. Glow, fade; glow, fade. One final explosion of heat and then crush. Stub out the cigarette in the ashtray. Done, forgotten.
Something causes him to smile. Living his dream. Living

his dream to the butt end. The disposable, discardable moment before neglect; before the death of memory. His foot twitches; he can see the shadow of a path before him.

'So,' he says aloud. 'This is it. The final burst. This is the end. The beginning of the end. This is the penultimate moment.'

Click.

Flame.

Inhale.

The doorbell rings.

His cock is in Niente's ass. Niente does not know how it got to this stage but his cock is in his ass. He pounds. Pushes deep, it feels good. Niente knows it should not be this way but it works. He feels like he has known him for years, like he should have known him. This feels right. Everything about it feels right. Like it should have been. *It should have been.* It never happened. It is happening now. It is the second time. Niente has already shot his load in him.

*Flashback.* A memory that cannot exist. Shooting a load in his ass on the floor of his friend's house.

*Now.* He is pushing deep. 'Sorry,' he says.

'What?'

'Nothing.'

He fucks Niente harder. Bent into a V, he is tugging at his own cock, stuck against the headboard and his body. Fuck. Fuck. Fuck.

'I'm gonna cum,' the stranger breathes. His face screwing up. Each thrust harder, faster. Then bang. One final slam and he cums with a scream. It erupts out of nowhere and Niente shoots his load as a result. The stranger's cock and cum planted deep inside. They collapse in a sweaty, out of breath mess. Two forms entwined on one bed. Naked flesh glistening. Niente's legs locked around him, preventing him from pulling out. Warm all over. No one says anything. They let the moment soak into them. It feels like they have been waiting a million years for this.

The cigarette burns between Niente's fingers. He lies in bed, the stranger next to him, head against his shoulder. *What am I doing?* he thinks. He does not know but it feels right. Too right, like it is meant to be. For this one moment he feels complete. *How can I have memories of someone I've never met?*

The stranger stirs and reaches for the cigarette. Inhale; exhale. He smiles. There is love in his eyes. Niente can tell it is mirrored back. 'Hey,' the stranger says. 'I don't even know your name.' A laugh.

Niente chuckles, names seem irrelevant at the moment. 'I guess you're right.' The introduction is not made. They kiss instead.

Another fuck later and they emerge naked from the bedroom.

'Don't you feel it too?' the stranger asks. 'Nothing has been the same since that meeting. Nothing feels right, except *this*.'

'I don't get it though. How can we share memories? I've never met you.'

'Maybe we were meant to meet but never had the opportunity.'

'What, so they're like a parallel universe cross over?'

'Well, maybe not like that.'

Niente laughs, at least he has a sense of humour. 'Cup of tea?'

'Yeah, sure.'

Niente boils the kettle. He does not turn around. 'So why did you really come here?'

'What?'

'I mean you didn't go through all that effort to stalk me just for a fuck and love at first sight bullcrap. So, what do you want?'

The stranger swallows. Sweat beads at his temples. 'I believe I have to do something.'

'What?'

'I had a dream.'

Niente spins around. 'Dream? What kind of dream?'

'They showed me my destiny, the future. This was it. To show you a memory from your past. Your memory will be imprinted with one of mine. The vision will be complete.'

'But how can it be "complete"? I don't know you.'

'I have to show it. Then I will leave. Please.'

'Do you want this tea then?'

'Maybe something stronger.'

'Like what?'

The stranger drops his eyes to Niente's track marks. He flicks his eyebrows and takes a deep breath. Ready to word he opens his mouth. Niente saves him the effort.

*Memory.*

The snow falls out of season. White. Niente walks down a path, a line of trees to his right, to his left open field. The snow is thick, it grinds under his feet. With one hand in his coat pocket, the tips of the other prickle with the cold as they hold a cigarette. A Marlboro Gold Menthol.

He is pissed off. Walking away from something. He does not know what, but he is changing something, an emotion, a moment. Moving towards the present. He knows what is going to happen. He has been here enough times. Always the same. Never ending. Why do they not just end it and be done? *Fucking dickhead.*

Niente can see his boyfriend standing there in the distance, he makes no move to help close the gap between them. Niente is to blame; he has to make all the effort. *As usual.* Niente stops a few paces in front of him. They do not make eye contact. 'Hi,' Niente offers.

'So?' his boyfriend Anthony spits.

'What?'

'So what do you have to say?'

'What do *I* have to say? *You're* the one who changed his mind and didn't go out.'

'And you think it's all right to punish me by not telling me what you were doing? You could have been doing anything with anyone.'

'Oh fuck off! So I have to edit my life around your constant mind changes? You can't stop me going to enjoy myself. *And* thanks for your considerably low perspective of me.'

'Get over it.'

'No, you fucking get over it.' Niente spits his words with as much acid as he can muster. 'Fuck it. If you're gonna be a dick do it on your own time.' He throws his arms up into the air, his eyes rolling a 'fuck you' as he turns and begins to walk back the way he came.

The silence is painful. Ahead of him a couple run across the snow. Play fighting. They hug. One is wrestled to the ground; he pulls the other after him. Making out. Niente watches the scene, brought to a halt by its beauty. *That should be him,* he thinks, *that could be me.* That should be Anthony and himself. This petty shit is not worth losing out on possible moments like that. Maybe they *can* make it work.

He turns around. Anthony a disappearing form. He does not even look back. *Why am I even trying?* Niente runs after him. *I try because I care.* Anthony ignores Niente's calls. *Why do I do this?* He catches up and places his hand on Anthony's shoulder. *Is this worth it?* Anthony turns and looks at Niente with tear-soaked eyes. *I know why I do it.* They embrace each other. *Love.* Niente's eyes stare blankly into the distance. *Why am I doing this?*

Static burst. His vision clears. Seeing through eyes that are not his own. A brain trying to fight for its own dominance.

Snow, thick. It clings to the land. A blanket to hide reality for a fleeting moment. A figure. A black silhouette moving away. Shrinking. Never once looking back.

The figure disappears from sight. He does not move. He cannot move. *I'll wait some more.* Two trains pass by. He is going to be late but he does not care; this moment is too great. *This is the moment when…*

Two figures run across the snow. Fight, hug. One is wrestled to the ground. He pulls the other down with him. *That's it. That's it, all over.* The couple continue to move as a pair. *I'm happy for you, I really am, but I wish that was me.*

*I want that to be me.*

He stands and waits. The third train passes. He cannot pull away. His eyes just focused on the happiness taking place in the distance. Locked on the beauty before it, the future watches and the present succumbs to the past.

*Present.*

One opens the door to his flat. Three hours ago he was meant to have walked into work but he did not. His routine changed and nothing was the same. It all seems pointless, his old life. Work, work, work. How is that satisfying?

He throws his keys onto the kitchen unit and pours himself a glass of wine. The telephone rings. He lets the machine answer. Work. They sound pissed. *Shit happens.* He takes a sip and manoeuvres his body into the living room and throws his dead weight onto the sofa. *Fuck.* He hopes Niente will do as he said and hold up on his word. *Something isn't right.*

*There.*

One creeps down the staircase. Slowly, as quietly as he can. The lights flicker, their naked bulbs dimming to a pale orange, it illuminates nothing, letting the shadows in. They huddle in the corners biding their time, planning their moment.

He stays in the dull glow and continues to the living room. He pushes the door open and peers in. His parents sit in the darkness. The only light the white from the static filled television screen. Father's hand rests on the remote yet he does not change the channel. Mother says nothing. Neither say anything.

He steps through the door, his foot does not connect to the floor. He stops it short when he sees it. The single tear of blood running from their noses. The overwhelming emptiness that fills the room, personified by the shadow standing in the corner. Tall, gaunt, tendrils of smoke rising and falling elegantly around it. He slams the door on the scene.

One runs down the hallway, it stretches further than it should. The lights sway above his head, stretching the shadows across his path. The door opens behind him and the emptiness slicks its way through.

His feet slow. He—

Bright light. White. Surgical. It casts no shadows across the white landscape. Both land and sky the same colour. The merging of heaven and earth in a glorious disorientation of all the senses.

He turns. His eyes fall upon it. A circular tower of steps leading up to a throne. The figure sat upon it slumped and in shadow, the only shadow. He walks towards it. The noise begins. A dirty sound, a bass pitch. Vibrating; swirling. Its rhythm at odds with the scene. His body slows. It saps his energy, pulls at him. He begins to climb, the pressure dragging him down. With a sigh he collapses at the last step. Using the last of his determination to turn round.

All he sees is white. The sky. The throne and its figure hidden from his line of sight. He can sense its darkness. It fills the air like an emotional perfume. His eyes close. He has failed. That was not the conclusion.

*Reality.*

They walk the streets. Twilight, a day wasted fucking. Niente still doesn't know the stranger's name. Some things are so trivial against a raw emotion. He feels drained. *When did life become this fucked and broken?* Ever since that day in the graveyard. One snowflake changed everything.

This is life; a stumbling series of unplanned encounters pulling you towards a goal. Paths untaken linger as parallels, what ifs, regrets.

Live without regret, a route not taken has no substance on which to impact a future.

Niente looks at the intimate stranger. How can a route not experienced create memories in two minds? How can feelings feel so strong as though it was always meant to be? So many questions, they blur, spiral around his thoughts and then he zones out.

'This is me.'

Snap awake. 'What?'

'This is where I live.'

'Oh.' Niente looks at the path leading to the door. 'Okay.'

'So… erm…' The awkward moment. The life changing moment. This is where destinies can be built or torn asunder. A split second to lead to new places. 'Yeah.'

Niente shakes his head. 'I'm okay. I need to head off and get some rest. It was nice meeting you. Fucked, but nice.'

'Yeah.' The awkward hug and hesitated peck on the cheek. 'Maybe we can go for a drink? Whenever you're free.'

'Yeah sure.' The awkward exchange of phone numbers.

'Okay then.'

'Okay then.' The awkward wave. 'See you soon.' The awkward walk away. Should he look back over the shoulder or just keep going? Niente just keeps walking. His heart breaks with emotion that should be nonexistent. This is the end of that choice. Life must go on and this meeting has helped him realise that. He must solve it. The unknown problem with its impossible solution. The truth is just a perception of a mind. Reality is 'truth', just a perception. Perceptions can be changed. Something clicks in his head, a switch flicked and fuse blown. No going back, no looking back. No regrets. This is it. Roll on the grand finale.

His feet stop. He stands in the middle of a roundabout. He turns full circle. Houses. Each house flickers blue. One window filled with blue flashes, the others blackened portals to different worlds. They stand in silence. Ghosts. Memories. They pull him towards them. He moves towards a window, through the gate and down the path. Through the glass he sees. The figure sat in the chair, hand poised on remote. The shriveled fingers do not move, do not twitch. Its eyes stare blankly at the static on the screen. No movement. No sound. Niente knocks on the window. The figure does not even blink. Focused on eternity.

Next house. New window. They lounge cuddled together on a sofa. Lovers, entwined in their embrace. The static reflects off their dead eyes. He knocks. They remain focused on eternity.

Niente breaks into the third house. He walks his way though the quiet hallway. Its darkness illuminated by the blue from one room. He opens the door wider and steps across the threshold. The figure is knelt in front of the television set. The remote held out by one arm, finger about to change the channel. She does not move, he knows she will not.

A step closer and he sees the blood trail from her nose, dried crimson. Her eyes stare at the static for eternity.

Niente sits in an armchair. Staring at the frozen figure. *Why is this happening? Why is it happening to me?* He closes his eyes. Counts to five. Opens them. The scene remains the same. This is no dream. This is reality. *Die in my world or find me in yours.*

*So,* he thinks, *if you can exist in both, why can't I?* He empties his mind. Relaxes back and stares slack-jawed at the television screen. His vision blurs, refocuses, blurs. Darkens. Tendrils of smoke rise from the floor, the paint curls on the wall. The girl rots, her face decays to a husk. The shadow moves in from the corner. Its soundtrack follows it. The noise, the dirty noise that has haunted his dreams. It touches the girl and she explodes in a fountain of ash, it falls around him like snow.

He tries to move. The shadow turns to him. Tall, gaunt. Ancient. Its darkness opens like a mouth and it screams. The divine scream. The voice of judgment. Then it explodes. Erupts into thousands of flies. They surround Niente, blinding him, forcing their way into his ears, his mouth, down his throat. He claws at his mouth, trying to make space for a scream to exit. He chokes. Panicking he jumps to his feet.

The girl still stares at the television. The channel remains unchanged.

# CHAPTER TWELVE

*Memory.*
Niente scoops up the pills and puts them into his pocket. He leaves his room. In the kitchen he opens a cupboard and takes out a bottle of vodka. He has everything he needs. As he closes the front door behind him he hears his phone chime with a new message. He does not care.

His feet guide him towards the graveyard. A perfect place to end it all. Silent, peaceful. The dead can help guide him into their world. An abandoned soul released on consecrated ground. He smiles, he likes the beauty in that. There is always a beauty in death.

At his destination he finds a place and sits down. With his back against a tree at the heart of the graveyard he looks at the moss-covered stone slab in front of him. He wonders what his will read. He takes another swig from the bottle he had already started drinking on his way. One last time to think. One last moment to contemplate. His mind wandering within its own wilderness. *What the fuck is there for me anymore but pain and this hollowness? Just going through the motions of living until the day nature decides I die. Why should my life be in anyone's hands but my own?*

He is lost. Lost his direction, lost his way. His mind can see no future, *wants* no future here on this earth. He has dreams but none have been powerful enough to let him make that choice. Something has to end; rather than break the heart of the one he cares for through rejection, he has decided to be the something that dies. The end of every single dream, hope and love he has ever felt or known. It is time for him to embrace the shadows and be reborn as someone else. Inside he is dying, losing. He feels the pills in his pocket weighing his mortal body down like an anchor. He prays that salvation will come through taking them. He swigs from the bottle. The first two are swallowed.

Will they all forgive him when his candle fades? Will they understand? Could they? All he wants is freedom from all this pain; he wants peace, a mind freed from insecurities and self-loathing. All he had ever asked for was a simple answer, an acknowledgment that he had a reason to be here, that he was valued, not just humoured. All he wanted was to have found his place in the world. He swallows another pill.

All he hears in his head is screaming. Voices upon voices screaming at him, putting him down, killing him. Rotting all his confidence and pride to nothing, causing him to self-destruct. Too many demons clawing at his back, too many painful memories. Too much anger and deceit. Can he blamed for wanting to end all that? He gulps the vodka; no pill this time.

All he wants is to be someone else, someone different. Someone new. To be born again with new hopes, new situations, no memories to hold him back. When he looks at himself he sees a sickness, bitter thoughts and remembered words clinging to his soul like cancerous tumours. Eating away at everything, growing daily. Is it wrong to want to be free from pain? His world is killing him slowly, now he is just taking control.

His mouth opens. 'Come on then,' he screams into the dark. 'You said you'd been waiting for this moment. Waiting to consume me. Well don't miss the finale.' He cries, sobs painfully. 'This is what you wanted. This is what *you* wanted. This is what *I* wanted.' His voice breaks to a whisper. 'Is this what I wanted?'

His eyes close. A single tear rolls down his cheek. *Is this what I wanted? I'm nothing... I'm nothing... I'm nothing but worthless dirt.*

He senses movement, a darkening of the scene. His eyes open and he sees the shadow, standing three gravestones back. Tall, gaunt. Tendrils of smoke rising and falling around its base. Niente swallows. Blinks. Rubs his eyes, but the shadow does not fade from sight. It stands there, waiting.

Scrambling to his feet, Niente takes an unsteady step towards it. Then another. Then another. His head starting to feel thick from the alcohol. 'It's you,' he offers, his voice wavering. 'It's you from my dream.'

'I do not belong to you,' the shadow whispers, its voice a low growl. 'I do not belong to anyone.'

Niente finally reaches the shadow; he stares up at its featureless face. 'Who are you? What are you?'

A beat. The silence engulfs his words before the shadow speaks. 'I have watched you from a child. I have seen you grow, seen what you have endured. I am the darkness from which you were born and the darkness at your end. I am eternal. You have felt my presence all your life, in every decision you have made. You and I, we are fated together.'

Niente frowns, confused. 'Why are you here?'

'Am I not what you wanted to see? In your dreams I gave you advice, tried to make you see. I need you. The darkness needs you.'

'Needs me?' Niente smirks. 'Who am I? I am nothing. I'm a nobody.'

'Everyone is special in their own lives, you are not the only one destined to reach achievements, but you need the courage to believe in your importance. Not everyone is chosen to achieve majestic levels, but you are one of the lucky ones. You are a power piece, not just a pawn.' The shadow pauses. 'Oh, such confusion in you. So lost. So alone in your self-conceived wretchedness that you deny yourself an existence. I can see the end points of your journey. I see your final resting place. I see the whole stretch of life in front of you, the infinite parallels. Your path, no matter the route, converges at the same point. Remember what will be asked of you.'

'Asked of? By who?'

The shadow laughs. 'Such sudden impatience from someone who only moments ago prayed for the end. You will know when the time comes and you will fight it. Let me tell you one thing. All this is a lie.'

'What's a lie?'

The shadow begins to move away. It does not answer.

'What's a lie? You? I don't understand.' Anger enters his voice. 'Why won't you answer?'

The shadow turns sharply towards him and roars. Its frame explodes into thousands of black flies. They swarm towards him chaotically; as they rush past he feels it. Anger, rage, a never ending loneliness pouring from them. The kiss of eternity against his skin. The birth and loss of everything, the darkness, the silence. They fade into the distance behind him.

Niente jolts up. The graveyard lit by the glow of dawn. The first touches of sunshine awakening. He pulls himself to his feet, pulling his coat tighter around him. He feels the world turn beneath his feet, sees the shadows moving in the corners. Something stirs within him. A fire, a desire. Something stirs in the darkness. The end days are in motion.

He looks up into the clouded sky to see the first flake of snow fall.

# CHAPTER THIRTEEN

He lies on the bed, his eyes staring blankly at the ceiling. His phone rings. He ignores it. The machine answers for the fifth time since he has been home. *So this is what Niente feels,* One thinks. *This is his calm in all the madness in his head. His escape from his daily pain.* He smiles. The belt still hangs loose around his arm. *I bet I look a mess.* He does not really care. Euphoria after the pain of his dream. The same dream reoccurring in his mind. *Who sits at the top of those stairs?* Will he ever find out? Then there was *that* dream. The shared dreamscape. What he learnt.

A tear runs from his eye. He misses Rose. It is a silent mourning. Niente will never know what they had shared, he must never know. Those nights of passion, of holding each other, they would eat at Niente's core. The secrets of his best friend. That morning he sneaked out of the door as Niente lay in a drug stupor. The night Rose had called him to the club after Niente's worst mental freak out. The secret leading away of his broken-hearted boyfriend. These are things Niente needs to be shielded from. His fragile mind would snap more than it already has. They kept it a secret to protect him.

*Who am I trying to kid? We did it to protect ourselves.* And now Rose has gone. Freed herself from this world and leaving One with all the guilt. All the secrets piled onto his shoulders.

He sighs, sits up, rests his head in his palms. Should he tell Niente that he had spoken to her on her last morning? The morning she sounded dead inside. Stalked to the point of oblivion by her nightmares. The crumbling of her life. The changes Niente had helped her see. *They* had experienced it, One was just the outsider. Their disconnection had allowed them to see cracks, cracks he had dismissed as mere addiction. *Is this why I did this? A replacement? To try and see? To try and help?* That dream comes to his mind. What had the fortune-teller meant? What did anything mean? *What is happening to me?* He thinks about how easy it was to find the heroin. All he had to do was go to where they had told him; he stole the syringe and needle from work. He looks down at himself, then leans his head back with sigh. He corrects his head and looks across his room to the blank wall opposite. He likes the way the glass shatters as it connects with it.

Niente still stares. The daylight filtering through the curtain-less window illuminating the scene with undiluted clarity. The girl knelt before him. Her back to his existence, staring lost into a dead channel. There is no soundtrack to life other than what we create. The true sound of the universe is the silence of mortality. *What's happened here? What's happening? Why's it happening to me?* He is done with emotions. He is done with the fear of the unexpected. The unexpected keeps happening; it is routine. It is life. *His* life.

A sigh. It breathes out from deep within him; it exits into existence and evaporates on a dead scene. He is the only living entity in the room and even he does not feel alive. A comedown, the merging of realities within a nightmare. He opens the bag he always carries and pulls out his rig. He injects his life back into his veins.

There needs to be an ending. The time has come for such. A night sky oversaturated with prayers of pain, screams of the unknown. Millions of voices searching for meaning amongst the complexities of existence. Answers never satisfy. Conclusions can be argued. The end is just that. Finality. The opening of the gates. The journey's end. He knows that is what is coming, approaching from all angles. The end of his journey. Only one change separates angles from angels.

This is his ending. He is the chosen messiah to find out some truth that will illuminate a golden Ark of Testimony. Alone. He has to go the final stages all alone. That is how all this begun. That is how it will end. Alone, a needle in his vein. Another sigh. He pulls himself to his feet.

'Right bitch,' he says aloud. 'I'm coming to find you.'

He walks towards the television. He switches it off.

*There.*

The room burns white. Whiter than the blinding glare of the sun. There are no shadows here. Except for one. The shadow around the throne.

One's legs guide him. The usual route. A broken record. A broken dream. As he begins to rise he knows the ending. The non-conclusion. The fall. The failure.

He collapses one step from the top. Senses the shadow around him. Reaching out for him. He failed. This is not the conclusion. He blinks...

The room burns white. Whiter than the sun. Surgical. There are no shadows here. Except for one, two. The shadow around the throne, the shadow of burgeoning addiction on his arm.

His legs guide him. The usual route. He begins to rise; he knows the ending. The non-conclusion. The fall. The failure.

He collapses one step from the top. Senses the shadow around him. This is not the conclusion. He blinks…

The room burns white. Brilliant pure white. There are no shadows here. Except for one, two, three. The shadow around the throne, the shadow of burgeoning addiction, the shadow jading his mind.

His legs guide him. The usual route. He begins to rise; he knows the ending. The non-conclusion. The fall. The failure.

He turns. Changes the path. He outstretches his arms and jumps. Casting a fourth shadow, he sees it against the land through tormented eyes.

He falls.

'Wake up,' says the old, wizened female voice. It breaks the dream like cancer.

*Reality.*

Niente rises from the Underground. He knows this station well. Waterloo. This is an exit. It has to be. The people rush around the immense space of the station. Pausing only to look at screens. A number change and off they rush. Always seeking a destination other than the one they are in. Escaping the city. Escaping the stage.

All independent. All different.

The station calms. He hears the rumble of the Tube below him. The rats pour from the sewer. The same faces. All independent. All different.

*What?*

Niente focuses. Tries to piece the scene together. He breathes, concentrates. A train passes below. The rats run. He focuses on a blonde-haired woman. Early forties, power-suited to importance. She walks quickly. Pauses. A number changes, she heads away out of sight.

Ten minutes pass. A train rumbles below. The sewers bleed. He focuses, the blonde-haired woman. Early forties, power-suited self-importance. She walks quickly. He follows. He watches the screen from beside her, she does not notice his existence. He is a ghost, or is she? Her eyes stare blind. Glazed. Lifeless. Just an extra on a film set. Cheap. Forgettable. The number changes. They walk off towards a platform.

They approach. All of a sudden, crowds are pushing him back. Blurred visions with no definite features. Unfocused, unable to focus on. The woman cuts through them as clear as a ray of light. The torch through a mist of the unknown. He tries to follow. The crowd pushes him back. The more he struggles, the quicker they move, the louder their mumbles.

He strains his ears. 'Go home,' they whisper. Hundreds of people repeating an order. No way through.

Ten minutes pass, the woman walks smoothly, expertly through the crowd. He makes to follow. All paths blocked. No way forward. The message changes his thoughts. 'Go home.'

Maybe he should go home. Maybe this is just his stupid drug habit. Nothing but a dream. He will wake up shortly. Either a deep sleep or a coma. Either way he will wake up. In dreams we sleep. In reality we exist. One day he will just wake up again.

The woman walks through the crowd. The blurred say

'go home.' He turns and returns to the sewers of existence.

He walks towards the entrance to the underworld. The woman walks past him. He follows her with his eyes. A number changes; she disappears from sight. He descends.

*What the fuck is happening?* he thinks, his mind heavy, a phantom hand squeezing his brain. A flash of blonde. He turns to see the power-suit rising away towards the light. He frowns. His bag slips on his shoulder. He pulls the plastic bullet from his pocket. Tilt, tap, twist. Sniff. One bump of ketamine up his nose. He rubs his nostril. Repeats the motion. A second bump enters his system.

*Right, fuck this. Home. This is pointless.* He needs time. He is just in trauma after the loss of Rose, of everything. It is just another breakdown. Another system reboot.

*There.*

Niente stands staring at a television screen. The remote in his hand. He does not change the channel. Brain dead. No ability to make a choice of its own, *his* own. He feels something drip from his nose. Tastes iron.

*Reality.*

He jumps back. A drop of blood falls from his nose. *Fuck.* Niente wipes away another and tries to stop the flow. His mind clear for one moment. Time pauses, the rats swarm around him but he remains locked in a bubble, his bubble. He came for a reason. *To find that bitch. To end this. To change, no, create an ending. To find the answers.*

He sees the woman advancing towards him. He swallows. Deep breath. He looks down at the shadow of his path, see hers cross into his. He reaches up and grabs both sides of her head. One sharp twist snaps her neck. She falls limp to the floor. He continues along their merged paths. He crawls out from the sewer, his fellow rats rubbing past him as though he was one of them, chattering excitedly amongst themselves.

He pauses below a screen. The number changes. He walks to the platform. No crowds rush towards him. No barriers block his path. He steps onto it.

# CHAPTER FOURTEEN

He walks along the empty platform. It stretches away, pinpointing in the distance, never opening into daylight. Weeds grow between the tracks of the empty platform to his left. The train on his right rusting through neglect. Its carriage filled with people, seated. Still, staring across from each other like waxen mannequins, the only evidence of their once living existence is the dried blood patch under their noses, a river born from one nostril and long since dried and lost to memory.

Niente presses his hand against the glass coffin, runs it against it as he walks towards the shadow of his destination. He presses the button to open the door without thinking. It grumbles open with a compressed sigh. He walks in to see the populace rot in front of him. Disturbed from their acrid air with that of change. The skin peels from their skeletons, curls and erupts into the air like the ash of a crematorium. It fills the carriage and he breathes in the death of sixty-two. He does not recoil; it filters up his nose as smooth as cocaine.

He plucks a newspaper from a hand and reads the date on its masthead. 23 July 2104. The day time stopped. The day the dreams ended.

In silence he walks the length of the carriage. It takes two minutes. Quite fitting. *When you stand in silence, pray your dreams will come.* The door whispers open around him. He steps back onto the platform.

He walks until the spacious surroundings shrink around him into a mere corridor. White walled. Strip lights overhead. Caked in grease and decay, their bulbs flickering intermittently. In the flicks of black the shadows dance to the music of his footsteps. He pays them no attention. No second thoughts. He just walks with purpose. *This isn't right.* It does not feel natural to him. *Find me in your world or die in mine.*

This must be the exit. The last station passed and now we travel blindly into the unknown. *Where are you?* he thinks. *Where the fuck are you?*

He hears a young girl laugh. It ripples around him. Echoes for a moment then disintegrates into silence. Humming. An innocent tune through a child's lips. Distractions are what he needs least but they comfort him from loneliness.

The corridor comes to an end. One solitary door, one way, no choice. The only way now is forward. He twists the handle. The door swings open. He steps through.

His flat. The door swings open and spits him out into his flat, slamming shut behind him. Niente spins full circle. *What the fuck?* He tries to exit through the door but it remains closed. Locked. No way. *Fuck.*

He walks to the kitchen and pours himself a glass of water. He senses movement behind him and he turns. It is that guy. The stranger. He smiles at Niente. Niente frowns. 'What? Erm… How?'

'What?' he looks surprised. 'I don't understand.'

'What the fuck are you doing here?'

'Oh thanks, like that is it?'

'I don't get it. You went home. I walked you there. What are you doing here?'

The stranger walks towards Niente and envelops him in an embrace. 'You stumbled out of bed for a hit; you didn't come back so I went to check on you. You'd passed out, I thought it best to let you sleep. You looked like you needed it.'

'What?' Niente looks at his arm. Sees a fresh needle mark, an hour old. *What?* He rubs his finger against it. When was his last hit? He did it at the girl's house. In front of the television screen.

An image in his head. Sat in front of his television. Staring at the static, breaking the skin with a needle prick.

A shake of his head and he is back in the room. He pulls out of the grip of the stranger. He rubs his hands down his face. 'So why's the front door locked? Where are my keys?'

'Here.' The stranger pulls them from his pocket. 'You told me to keep them safe in case you tried to get out during the night.'

*Makes sense.* It would not be the first time he had done that. He wants to cry. Wants to slam his head against the brick wall that is constantly in front of his face. *What's happening to me? I've cracked. Finally cracked.* He tries to control his brain, to maintain his world, his existence. He laughs. Of course it was all a dream, like anything like that could really happen. Calm. He feels calm.

'You look like shit.'

'Thanks.' Niente pours another glass of water.

'No seriously you do. Maybe you should take another nap.'

'Maybe I should.' Niente smiles. Gulps more liquid.

Places glass down on the counter and walks to the living room. The television is dead. No life statics across its screen. He looks at the rig on the floor. He frowns. The needle is discarded by the left hand side of the armchair as he faces it. He sniffs the air. Subtle change. Not massive, just enough to alienate his sanctuary.

'So I blacked out yeah?'

'Totally.' The stranger stands at the door. 'I was a bit scared at first. Thought you might have overdosed.'

'Funny.'

'What is?'

'How good you are at lying.'

'What?'

'Stop it.' Niente spins round. 'Just fucking stop it.'

The stranger takes a step back. 'Hey, calm down. What have I done?'

Niente reaches for the needle off the floor, quickly throwing it at his intended target. The stranger does not have time to move out of its path. It rips his skin and hangs limply in his arm.

'What the fuck are you doing you nut job,' he shouts. He pulls out the syringe.

'Get the fuck out of my house. I don't know who you are, or what you want but just get the fuck out.'

'Calm down. You're just spaced out. That's all.'

'Yeah so spaced out that the needle falls to my right.'

A frown. 'What?'

'I'm left handed you jackass. My needle always falls to my left. You would only know that if you'd spent the whole day with me. So since you did and you don't know, that makes you a fucking lie. A stranger in the body of another.'

Silence.

'So are you going to fuck off?'

'You think you're so fucking special. Do you think that you could achieve anything? Look at yourself in the mirror. You're twenty-eight, Niente, what have you got?'

'That's it.' Niente lunges at the stranger. He retreats to the bedroom. The door slams. 'Open this fucking door. I'm gonna fucking kill you.' No reply from inside. He bangs his fist against it. 'Open it now you fucking runt.'

Silence.

Niente kicks. The door breaks on its hinges. He rushes in, the scene changes.

Niente stands at the bottom of the flight of stairs. He knows exactly where he is. The Black Cap. Just the place he needs. *What the fuck is happening?* His world falling apart brick by miserable brick. He climbs the stairs, two at a time.

The place is full. He walks over to the bar and waits to order, ignoring those around him, their conversations just vacuous waste against his problems. He orders. He pays. He picks up the pint and turns. He sees.

The stranger and Anthony. Close as lovers. The stranger catches his attention. 'Sorry about earlier.' He approaches, hand outstretched in a gesture of friendship, reconciliation.

Niente pushes on with his walk and looks at the hand. He smirks, looks up at the head it belongs to. He spits right into its face. 'Stay the fuck away from me.' He turns to his ex-boyfriend. 'You can have him. He's just my discarded waste. Enjoy.' He leans in close, close enough to kiss. 'Welcome to the Hep C generation.' Niente turns on his heals; feels everyone's eyes upon him. 'What?' he shouts. 'You want a spectacle?' The pint glass smashes into some old man's face, shattering as it does. In the stunned pause, Niente makes his dramatic soap opera exit.

He grips the doors. He needs fresh air. It might help clear the noise in his head. Push open, step out. The corridor. *That* corridor. *What?*

The girl's laughter echoes down it.

'So, you think this is funny do you?' Niente shouts. 'You think this is fucking funny?'

A shadow at the end of the corridor. It stands waiting. The shadow of a girl. 'What are you waiting for?' she says, her voice cancerous and old. 'I have been waiting so long for this moment.'

Niente makes to run at her but his legs will not move. Struggling to pick up any form of speed no matter how hard he tries. Running through tar. He looks down. The floor is covered with inky shadows, their arms gripping on to him. 'Go home,' they whisper. 'Go home and forget all about this. Go home to save yourselves.'

'What?' Niente's attention is torn. The shadow or the shadows? *Who's right? Who's more important?*

'Go home.'

Niente turns to move. The journey back quicker. Easier.

'Do not go.' The girl's voice cuts through. 'Giving up on something so soon? How unlike you.' He hears an intake of a cigarette. 'What have you learnt through all this? The past is surely just the easiest option.'

Niente does not turn back to face her. 'Why so friendly? Why this air of friendship? You're a bitch. A dirty rotten bitch. I know what you did to Rose.'

'Oh really? She told you?'

'She didn't need to. I could see it in her eyes. You killed her. Killed her from the inside. You're poison. Why should I do anything *you* ask of me?'

'Because it is your destiny. Whether you like that fact or not, you know it is true deep down. You even went so far as murder for it.'

'That woman was a ghost, a figment of my imagination. This is all a dream. *You* don't exist.'

'That woman was alive and you killed her. She was a real as both you and I. So, is her life now just lost in vain just because you had a change of heart? Just because you have decided ignorance is bliss? You are weak. You disgust me.'

'You fucking bitch,' Niente roars. He races down the corridor towards her. The shadows do not touch him.

The girl smiles as she lifts the glass of vodka to her lips. 'Such determination. Such lust for something. Now that is what I like to see in a man.'

# CHAPTER FIFTEEN

The snow falls around him. Black snow. Falling like the ash of angelic abandon. The girl stands beneath a dead tree. Hip cocked, cigarette in one hand, glass of vodka in the other. She must only be twelve.

Niente advances. As he closes the gap between them she offers him a cigarette. He takes one, lights it with his own lighter. Click, flame, inhale. 'So?' he questions before exhaling.

'This is it, the ending. The final moments.'

'I guess so.' He looks around. 'I'm dreaming still, right? This is a hallucination. A K hole, or have I finally gone and overdosed?'

'I can assure you of one truth and that is that this is all *very* real. You are as awake as you ever are. If I cut you here, you will bleed in reality.'

'Where are we?'

'This is the Garden of Snow. *My* garden to which I am guardian.'

'Yeah, but where is it? Where are we?'

'The location does not matter. All titles are meaningless in the end.' She walks out from under the tree and catches the snow on her palm. 'This used to be a garden of dreams, of hope. They used to fall down like crystals; so pitifully fragile, so easily lost. The unfulfilled dreams of humanity stockpiled and waiting. Dying with each burning out of a mortal coil. That was when there was hope. The hopes became fewer. The garden died. Mankind had taken one step too far and the darkness fled from the shattered cracks and engulfed them. Soon a new snow fell. A new ash for a new angelic abandon. These were the screams of humanity, the empty prayers and lost cries of redemption. The gates of Heaven remained closed. The afterlife did not want the disease; did not want the filth of mankind. Too many souls unregulated would have led to revolution; mankind would have raped the afterlife as they had done when they were living. The Creator would not allow that. Humans were forbidden, not worthy of anymore second chances. Their souls remain locked in the infinity. The living dead perpetually in anguish. The garden bled their new collective unobtainable dream. This…' She outstretches her arms and turns full circle. 'This is the eternal pain of mankind. This is regret. This is the arrogant hope of a chance. This is your world.'

'I don't follow.' Niente's brain cannot process what is being said.

'This pile of ash is all that is left of your world. This is *it*. That and *you*. The last of your kind. Saved from divine intervention by nothing but luck. Chance. You were saved by your own ignorance. The darkness only took those who had a natural life path. You only had a fake; programmed and scripted by professionals. Everything you are is programmed. Your biography a synopsis. You survived and turned stale as you have nothing to guide you. Lost sheep endlessly needing a shepherd to lead them.'

'What?'

'Let me finish.' She smiles warily. 'Ask your questions

then.' A sip. A drag. 'You were entertainment, your lives just ratings on a screen. When the darkness came, it took away your masters. The puppets finally had the chance to break from their threads, but they missed it in favour of continuing to exist through the repeated routines they had perfected over the years. You grew stagnant. Luckily, unlike their screams, humanity was not built to last. The implants in your heads began to fail, cut the system. The implants would die and for one blessed second they felt reality before the darkness claimed them. They had one second of pure truth, that is more than can be said for the rest of your parasitic race.

'Mankind is dead. It destroyed itself. It destroyed everything else. It killed like cancer. You are all that remains. You are the end.'

'The end? This all sounds too unreal. Mankind isn't dead. We can't be the last.'

'You are. 23 July 2104. The day time stopped. The day your world ceased to be. None of you noticed. We watched you exist as drones. We have always been watching, always waiting for our chance to claim you. Then it came. You. The introduction of your character twenty-eight years ago. Your life planned from birth to death years before your actual conception. When the last day came, and the broadcasts stopped, your drug usage increase. Unregulated you medicated yourself to existence. Your stimulated brain conflicted with your implant and you crossed the lines of reality. The world you dreamt of exists. The world you believed you lived in does not. You began to create the cracks that have allowed us in. Our killing began but you still hold the key to the end. You get the choice. The voice. You lead the action. You, my dear boy, get to decide the future of your kind. Choose the direction you want it to take.

'Do you let this torment continue or do you end it? Switch the control and power down the system. Do you maintain a lie or do you give the gift of truth to the blind?'

'How could I make that choice? How could you expect me to make it?'

'You will make it, of that I have no doubt. Why is it you? It was prophecy. Pre-planned by the universe out of human control. You are here and you alone must choose.'

'Life or death?'

'The age old classic.' She leads him by his arm away from the garden. She walks him towards the door that stands in a field of nothing. 'This is your life's moment. This is a destined goal. You should feel lucky.' The girl pauses. She holds her hand so the tree of the garden sits in it. 'Never believe just what you see, things may not always be as they seem.' She swings the hand towards him. The tree sits miniaturized in her palm, stolen from the distance. 'Remember the prophecy is plural. The leader is not always the decision maker by default. You hold the power of choice.' She opens the door with her free hand and gestures him in.

'Do I get to know your name?'

'My name is Cyan.' Cyan, such a cold colour, a colour of the dead.

'Cyan?'

'Goodbye.' Her hair whips around her in an invisible wind. She turns blacker, her form a silhouette. Her head cracks open and a flock of ravens fly into the sky, her body turns in on itself and spits out the last bird.

'Bye then.'

The door opens into a control room. The walls lined with multiple screens, flicking at regular intervals between locations. Locations he knows all too well. London. Its interior and exterior all filmed in constant high definition. He stares at the screens. The park, the coffeehouses where he has shared so many secrets. An endless scene change of familiarity. He stands transfixed for ten minutes. A screen changes, he sees his ex in bed with some unknown. Their sex is erratic, passionate. One rides the other, sweat beading on their skin. Feral, like wildlife documentary footage. He feels sick. A screen change. A camera focuses on the scene, the figures in the chair do not move. A dried trickle of red under their nose.

Screen change. Rose's flat. Empty. Set up as she last exited. Dead.

Screen change…

Niente rips his eyes away from the monitors. He feels empty. Confused. All meaning and understanding raped from his body. *What is this place?* He turns a half circle and sees the wall of filing cabinets. He moves to them, pulling the nearest drawer open. It contains files, all colour coded, all in alphabetical order. Two colours. Red and blue, the corner tabs names. He flips through them. They are familiar. He knows most of them for some reason. He pauses at his own and pulls it out. Numb he lets his body descend towards the floor and sit crossed legged. Spreading the file open in front of him.

He reads the opening lines.

NAME: *Niente Salvador Laing.*
DATE OF BIRTH: *23 February 2079.*

ESTIMATED LIFE-SPAN: *26 years.*
CHARACTER TYPE: *Main. Male. Red.*

PSYCHOLOGICAL PROFILE: *Dissociative disorder and Schizophrenia – symptoms of both present from the age of four onwards. Describes a longstanding unhappiness with his appearance and a sense of disconnection from himself and from other people.*

He reads his life. Key points bulleted for easy reference. Each main event planned, listed. Structured towards the conclusion. He reads the future that should have taken place. The exact date he should have finally met the stranger in person, two days after the end of time. 25 July 2104. The day his life was meant to change. The day it never happened.

He reads the future. He reads his unfulfilled death. He reads his pitiful existence and crumbles at what he became. How his own existence differed. The pain he had lived through for the past three years because everyone had lost their way. He does not cry. He cannot cry. He has no existence. He was just a main character.

He pushes the file away. Crawls to the cabinet on his knees, pulls out Rose's file, red. He reads about her affair with One, he reads the structure of her life, their meeting. Every argument and every break up. She was due to live until seventy.

One's folder is blue. He has read enough. He does not care anymore.

The next filing cabinet is filled with brown folders. The extras, the filling, all those lives without meaning; living generic lives just to create a sense of realism. A fake reality. Nurse 361. Waitress 67. Most did not even get a name; the background to the background.

Niente vomits. It hits the floor and soaks his file. He does not care. He does not care. He is nothing. He is nothing but a character. The tragic character. The one they all pity. The life destined to break. To end. To fade away amongst the happiness of normality.

On his feet he blindly walks towards another cabinet. It is labelled. This is what he needs to see. He pulls it open. Box upon box filled with small memory cards, catalogued by year and date, each listing the characters involved in each scene. He finds one hardcopy of his existence and pulls it out. One small piece of plastic encased circuit board is removed and he slots it into the system. A blank monitor fades into life. He stands and watches.

*Past.*

He stands against the door. The unknown male next to him. It was the first time they met. The first and only time. Together they walk into the bedroom of Niente's friend's flat. A friend lost to the following space of time. Her usage done she was written out of the series and discarded.

In the bedroom they are joined by others. Lines of speed go up one nostril; a frying pan of K is re-cooked in the kitchen. Lying on the bed everyone starts making out. Everyone getting off with each other. Touching. Kissing. Emotionless and empty. Niente pulls away from the stranger whose name he has forgotten. He does not want this. This is not why he is here. The guy pulls him in for another kiss. The K arrives as an intermission. More lines filter up the nose and everyone returns to the mass sexual contact. Three are already stripped to their underwear, drug flaccid cocks not even creating a noticeable bulge. Lips on his again and he slips a hand down the stranger's pants, falling into the scene, playing the role scripted for him.

He pulls away and someone new catches his eye. They connect. The episode's path changes. One-off character 30223 has his one meaningful exchange. Niente follows his beckoning, feeling like a child in need of protection. He pulls loose of the writhing bodies and climbs towards his saviour. They embrace in a hug. Comfort.

Ten minutes later Niente is sat hunched in a corner, a needle in his vein whilst all around him everyone fucks to a different orgasm. Aged eighteen this is his first cliff-hanger. He melts from existence. The episode ends. Roll end credits.

*Present.*
Niente remains in his position. The screen fades to black, a caption appears.

AUDIENCE APPRECIATION RATING: 100%.

It fades. The next episode begins. His brain refuses to process anymore of his past. Another monitor clicks to life. A repeat. Another past playing alongside his broken existence.

*Past.*
CHARACTER NAME: *David Thompson.*
CHARACTER TYPE: *Main. Male. Blue.*
David Thompson, father of three, husband of one. A pleasant existence upon the earth for almost five decades. He sits in his car, stuck in the rush hour traffic, already feeling his anger grow at his acceptance that he will be late for work.

*Bloody traffic.* To be fair it is not the traffic's fault today, he had been running late anyway, the occasional delays caused by family life. Wife ill, teenage children arguing over the breakfast table, the oldest did not even return home last night, not even a phone call.

He feels a smile cross his lips, how little things change. He remembers doing all that teenage rebellion when he was younger, just like his father had done, and his father's father. A generational repeat of turbulent adolescence. His smile drops, how did he get from that to this? When had those youthful dreams turned into adult ambition? You never stop to notice until it is too late. Here he is, half a century old; too old to break free from his regime, too blinded by the lure of money to dare risk attempting to fulfil the childhood fantasies of the past.

He slams his hand against the steering wheel. *The past is past; leave it there.* The traffic is not moving.

Lost in thought, the monotonous hum and grind of sardined cars fades into the background, he never has his stereo on, he hates the music, he hates the news. He would rather sit semi-patiently in silence, which is after all, as the saying goes, golden. He would much prefer to live in ignorance than worry about the world outside his cozy existence. His eyes watch the haze of rising exhaust fumes. Mankind still polluting the heavens, a toxic barrier to prevent the gods from interfering. Apparently once they had used notions of Global Warming as methods to try and change how people lived their lives, obviously they had not worked, nothing changed. The major fuel companies created synthetic chemicals to replace the fading fossil fuel reserves; these were just as deadly, if not more so. The climate was merely adjusting, once that nugget of information slipped out everyone stopped caring and the world turned and grew dirtier.

In his car David Thompson snorts, a disgusted smirk flicks across his lips. One hundred years ago they had used health scares and sensationalist news reporting to control the minds and actions of the nation, now it is simply brute force. Words replaced with violence; letters of warning exchanged for broken doorways and bullet stained walls. Fifty years upon the Earth and he had never seen a change in government. One party reigned supreme, one political party, the only party. The Council of Ten.

He smiles to himself, he does not truly care. He is comfortable, has a good job, a good home and a loving family, what importance is faith and dreams compared to that? He slams his hands against the steering wheel again. *Why isn't the traffic moving?* He is paid by the hour, if the traffic does not get going he will be losing money every second he is sat staring into the rear window of the car in front.

Slowly they inch forward, the traffic beginning to crawl past whatever is causing the hold up. Inch by inch they travel, the speed increasing. Ten more minutes pass before he sees the cause. A car crumpled against the railings of the road, another parked further down. The flashing lights of the police cars and ambulances flicker across his vision. As he passes he sees the body being pulled out from the wreckage. Limp, lifeless, dead. His lips curl into a snarl. He had been held up by someone's careless driving. How disgusting. How could they be so inconsiderate as to not think about the other users of this road? Thanks to them he is late, he will have to work his lunch break to make up the lost money.

Free from the traffic and with an open and well moving road ahead he puts his foot down and speeds off. At home the phone rings. His wife answers. Their oldest son has died in a car crash.

AUDIENCE APPRECIATION RATING: 78%

*Present.*

The Council's logo fades from the screen. Niente lets it imprint into his mind one final time.

The Council of Ten, their power won through revolution, maintained by force, funded by greed. All political opposition was removed and the people did not batter an eyelid, did not share a thought for the future generations. Democracy fell and the new era of tyrants began, nobody cried as the hard fought for freedoms vanished, nobody mourned democracy's death. They just applauded the new world order, applauded something they did not believe in.

The faiths had died, everyone just stopped believing. Science has all the answers; what use are gods when mankind believes it knows everything. Man's ego had grown, corrupted by its own self-importance. The heaven's power fell to the earth and they became the gods. A herd of cattle blindly following leaders because it was expected. When broken down to the basic level, mankind is just another herd animal, subservient to the alphas of their species.

This is what they did with that power. This is the divine pleasure of the gods. A digital amphitheatre. Slaves to the slaves. The pathetic lost sheep with their shepherds. Everything he knew was a lie. A deceit. A stone messiah to stimulate the masses. His entire existence a recreational anaesthesia ingested by the masses through their television screens. He struggled through life so they could sit in the comfort of their armchairs and 'share' his pain. He was nothing. His being created to plead to people's emotions. A warning, a message. His death would have sparked a national mourning. Millions crying to his synthetic demise. Then he would have been forgotten, his memory just repeats run when there was nothing better to view. He was a lie. He was...

He cries. He breaks down under the strength of emotions too impossible to comprehend, too much to process. He knows she stands behind him. He can smell the cigarette smoke. 'But what about me?' he howls. 'What about *me?*'

'Your feelings are real. During your life, for some reason, you broke down the implant's control over you. And as a result by the point the world ended, you had complete individual control; you have lived for three years as yourself, doing what you chose to do completely.' Smoke passes by his ear. He feels her stale breath against it. 'We let you experience, we needed you to.'

'But it's all based on falsehoods. A world created around me out of my control. I just continued in character. I changed nothing.'

'That is where you are wrong. You are what *you* created.'

Niente turns. 'What?'

Cyan stands as a hag behind him. Old, decayed, near death sullen face. She hands him his vomit stained file. 'You played your most important moment; did you read the file? You were not meant to take the needle. The orgy had been your storyline. You broke the plan and the show got its best ever rating. You changed the course of your destiny towards your nature; you did it again to get here. That is what you were destined to do. You are special, oh so special. The piece of fiction that can change the world; has the power to do so.'

'But humanity has gone. You said so.'

'Not all of it. You are the last of it in existence. The last or the first, the choice is yours.' She points to a switch. 'One flick of that and all the implants will fail. We will let everyone feel the touch of humanity for one minute. They will be free. The other option is to take over as god. To give meaning to the meaningless, to create rules and regulations by which people must adhere to be a part of your society. Mankind is lost in its own meaning and always has been. Enlightenment or the fall? It is your choice. You create the conclusion.' She turns from him. 'Your choice. You have all the time in the world to make it, but it will be made regardless. Bye Niente, we will never meet again.'

Cyan crumbles to ash before him. Dead. He knows that her existence has faded. The last hopes of humanity crumbling at his feet. Does he have the right to make that choice?

'Why me?' he screams, its pain tears his throat; it tears reality. 'Why the fuck does it have to be me? Why was I never given the change to just exist? To just be like everyone else. Why was I chosen to be broken?'

Only the damaged can help the damaged.

Eyes around the room. He sees an exit. The lift to reality. The real surface. The exit from the city. The last stop on the line. He gets in and makes his journey into the darkness.

Outside the sun burns down on the ruins of civilization. Nothing exists. Nothing lives. In one opening of a door Niente realizes, it comes flooding over him like a wave. There is nothing. The Earth was born from nothing; it is nothing. A spinning ball of hate and deceit created in the mind of slumber. It is all a dream, an idea, a passing thought. The darkness around it pressing in from all directions. All the dreams had been real, glimpses of the real world filtering through into his mind, mutated and empty. They had all died. They had all been discarded and removed.

The gods had not abandoned, they had been merely forgotten, pushed out of sight and left to rot as had everything touched by mankind. *Bored of you now, what's next?*

So, there are only two options. Their world could continue to turn, the dregs of mankind could continue to walk blindly through their programmed lives. No new thoughts, no progression, no future. It would naturally burn itself out over the years that would follow. Or it could all end. The exit has been planned; mankind has been given chances to save itself in the past, all of which were trodden on. This is the last chance for salvation. To wake from this dream and replace it with eternity. True eternity. The eternity born from the darkness. We are born from nothing and that is where we all shall return.

He looks out across the land and screams. It echoes out in the silence. His final cliff-hanger. The episode ends. Roll end credits.

# CHAPTER SIXTEEN

Niente paces the office. Everything in order, running according to plan. A perfectly organized affair being executed without flaw. He stops and looks out through the window, the decaying metropolis stretching far into the distance. He moves closer until his body can feel the breath of the glass. So this is his empire, this is his fate. Look into the veins of your nation whilst you sit at its heart.

A smile flickers across moist lips. A memory. It was a year ago that he had sat in that alleyway. It feels longer, like a different lifetime. In that place he had been reborn and now here he is. Soon he will be called for, summoned to go to the rally his government has organized, and being its Prime Minister, it is his duty to perform to the performers. To read aloud a speech he alone has the foresight will progress the story forward. He will provide order. New order after the destruction of the old. He snorts a chuckle to himself. 'Everything is circular,' he says to no one. 'The beginning our end.'

He returns to the depths of the room. Minimal and modern, if he had enough time he would change it, impress his mark upon it. Time, however, is always fleeting. From a drawer he pulls out a metal tin, cold in hand he falls back onto a sofa. Tin opens, preparation always the key. Heat the spoon, tourniquet the arm, tap the vein. Push.

Needle through paper skin, smooth as KY, the delicate whisper kiss of metal and flesh. Its warmth flowing through his vessels, as intimate a relationship as any unprotected lover. He leans back and locks his eyes upon the window again. One final trip. It is been said so many times before but this time he means it. Promise.

His body melts, dissolves to liquid and flows to the window. His soul follows, gliding across and out into the warm air. The glass smashes all around him, shattering into a thousand pieces, one for every life the Council of Ten had destroyed. They rain down bitterly onto the city. Payment for your apathy. Niente's soul escapes into the orange sky, the colour of pollution, the price of human advancement.

Deep below him the crowds passing look up. Glass falls like rain, several scream in agony, their eyes bleeding rivers of blood. Others smile, knowing. They all frown as a chair falls to the ground.

They slowly rise from the table; their designated time to leave for the rally had crept upon them. Grief stricken hands tapping out mournful rhythms. Mother walks to the mirror and adjusts her make up; hide your emotions behind a mask of your own creation. But such a weak mask, a solitary tear can do so much damage.

Father opens the drinks cabinet, one shot of bourbon burns away the salty taste of despair, or maybe it is the taste of disappointment, guilt. After all, his gun had been to blame. Another shot down his throat, he can feel the alcohol affecting his brain, numbing his pain, its dull thud distracting him from thinking too deeply. Alcohol, a blessing valued by so many. Much easier to run and hide than actually face your own demons. Father looks up; Mother has disappeared from the room. He knows where she will be, it has become routine.

He prepares his feet, one hand on the cabinet to steady himself whist the other brings the remainder of his drink to his lips. You cannot change the past but you can drown the sorrows it brings. He lets his feet guide him like a clockwork figurine, a life route plotted out and designated. When you have walked it so many times it loses its meaning. Today his heart beats like it had the first days after the shot, the hanging. Today was to be the start of something new, a national rebirth. It will be, only their number is down one.

He finds mother where he had anticipated, sat on the bed, her head buried in her hands. Her body shudders, the movement of silent grief. Each tear drop a memory evicting her body, soon she will be spent, feeling nothing but a dull thud in her heart. Today's rebirth will be the start of that.

Father moves through the door and sits beside her, his hand tenderly placed on her shoulder. 'It'll be okay, everything is going to be okay.'

Her head rises to look at him. Her make up has run, her mask cracked, she will need to touch that up before they leave. She whispers, 'But why? Why us?'

Father stares blankly, he does not know what to say.

'Why Tommy? If only he could have waited those two extra weeks.' A shadow of anger crosses her face. 'How could he do this to us? We gave him everything and this is how he repays us.'

Father squeezes her shoulder. Reassurance that he feels the same way. The inconvenience they had been put through because of him burns angrily through him. All that embarrassment, that shame, the questions just because he had had enough. Such a selfish way for their son to die. To die by your own hand reduces the sympathy they should be receiving for their loss. Father's lips snarl. 'The selfish bastard,' he says to himself.

She sobs next to him. Her body's vibrations shivering through the bed, her sorrow merging with the memories of countless joyous masturbations it has witnessed, strange that they both leave a salty taste on the tongue. Mother's arms reach around and grip onto Father. His hand brushes her hair. 'Why?' she repeats in a whisper. 'Why?'

He knows the question is not for him but he answers anyway. 'Maybe there is no logic to be found. No explanation.' Safe for the simple words he had written in his letter. 'We'll never know what he was thinking.' He rises from the bed, pulling free from her grip. He attempts to smile. 'Come on, we'll be late. It's an important day, everyone is going to be there.'

Mother stares blankly. 'Just a few more minutes,' she asks. 'Just a last goodbye.'

Father sits beside her again. What are a few minutes when today will be the beginning of better things?

The dead eyes of Tommy boy watch his parents as they embrace mournfully on his bed. He watches, his lips moving in silent prayer. They are going to be late, he knows that, but they will be forgiven because of their sorrow. Today is a big day for them, for him, for everyone. If only they knew. If only they could see what he had seen. His lips continue to move in silent prayer as his phantom body sways suspended from the ceiling.

*Memory.*

What do you do when you feel your life has achieved its meaning? That there is nothing more for you other than the slow countdown of days until the end. What are you to do? What can you do?

Tommy sits on his bed, his mind asking a constant stream of questions for which no answers come. His brain feels like a computer, endlessly calculating but never coming to a final conclusion, just clicking away for infinity, wearing itself down. How could he feel like this? He is only fifteen.

He rubs his face, got to hide the tears, boys are not meant to cry. But the pain, so much pain and for no reason. Inside he feels empty, spent. A battery that has lost all its energy. There has to be another way, another ending. There is only the darkness in his mind.

He lets the pen drop from his hand, it falls quietly on the bed. How are you meant to write what you feel when you feel nothing? The paper is dropped next to the pen and he allows his body to fall backwards, wishing the bed would melt away and he would simply disappear. The pillow greets him and the bed knocks gently against the wall. Think, close your eyes and think. Let images fill the mind's eye and disappear into your own world. His eyes close but only darkness awaits. He cannot focus, cannot dream. To dream is to have a future, and only the dead have no future to call their own.

A flash of blue, a line running across the closed eyes' field of vision. The darkness stretches off into the distance, he can tell. His eyes are not just seeing the closed flaps of skin, they are staring out into a void, a void of nothing, yet he can sense movement, faint glimmers of shadows, faces peering in to look at him. His ears ring with a hum, an electronic hum, wavelike, ebbing and flowing. Voices within the noise, a language unknown to him. So this is how it is to live without future. To face the darkness every night.

Tommy's eyes snap open. He sits up suddenly; gripping the pen he writes his final message on the pad. His epitaph, his final goodbye. Satisfied he smiles. A tear rolls down his face. He knows there is no future for him in this form. He knows because all his dreams had showed him as someone else, someone new, a life waiting for him after this. Then they had stopped. When the dreams had died he knew that the time had come. Redemption only a step away.

His parents were away for the weekend and the house was his. Alone no one could disturb him. He looks up, the homemade noose dangles from the ceiling, crudely constructed but its purpose would be served. He watches it sway, as if tempting him to feel its embrace. Something was stirring in the shadows, an uncertain future on the horizon, a bright and glorious fresh start. How he longs to be born again in that era of hope. In that new dawn he will have his meaning.

He rises from the bed, no second thoughts in his head. As he moves he picks up Father's gun, compact and easy to handle, everything has been thought through. There will be no future for this life.

He steps up onto the chair he set up under the noose. The gun is pushed partially into his jeans whilst he tightens the rope around his neck. He retrieves the gun; places its bitter nozzle into the mouth. With his eyes wide open he pulls the trigger, the bullet crashes through him, as he body crumples the chair gives way. In the few seconds before his spinal cord is severed he hears nothing but blissful silence.

*Present.*

Mother still sits on the bed; her body shakes in dry sobs, her tears spent. Lost and confused her mind refuses to accept her loss. With his arm around her shoulder, Father's mind remembers Tommy's last message, the note he has kept hidden away from Mother. Two simple words: *I'm sorry.* Fifteen years of care and all he could say was that.

Father rises from the bed and pulls his wife gently up with him. 'It's time to go,' he whispers tenderly into her ear.

'I know.' She smiles and nods. Making her way to her son's mirror she pulls her make up out of her purse. Time to reapply the mask, time to hide away the marks of grief. From her position she watches Father leave the room, a minute later she hears the distant clink of a whiskey bottle whisper through the house. She smiles as she places the pill on her tongue and swallows it dry. The bitter scrape the price for the Valium calm soon to follow. One final adjustment, one final check. She walks to the door and crosses the threshold. One final glance before she closes the door and retraces Father's footsteps.

He stands in the kitchen waiting. He holds out her coat and helps her into it. They embrace, a tender kiss. So many secrets between them, but so much love as well. They walk to the door and leave. Out of the corner of her eye Mother sees Tommy following in silence. She smiles softly. A family for one last time.

One paces his office, agitated. Everything is running to plan, all morning he has received an endless stream of updates telling him so, but still he is uneasy. Today is the day. It scares him how quickly it has rolled around, and who would have thought it? The Council had fallen and now Niente was here to take control. It had happened out of nowhere. The unexpected revolution. All it takes is one person to change a course of history.

One has not heard from Niente all morning, he is no doubt pacing his office like One. Something had changed though, One had noticed a difference in him, like he knew something, like he had seen something that had scared him. Maybe it was just the pressure of today.

He looks at the television screen, the news coverage on mute. His heart misses a beat; a chill shivers down his spine as his eyes take in the image. A discarded chair lying on the ground. Faces pouring blood through lacerated skin.

'Not today,' he mutters to himself. 'Please Niente, not today of all days.'

The camera pans up to see the pinprick shattered window high above the street. The screen smashes as One's chair hits it.

'You bastard!' he screams as he rushes from the room.

*There.*

Below him Niente can see the stretch of the city. Darkened at its core, overshadowed by the giant steel and glass fingers of progress. A nation hidden in shadows, hidden in greed. Corporate buildings stretch their rotten roots deep into the Earth. Directionless. He had never dreamt of this day, it feels so hollow. After everything he had witnessed how could such a sight fill him with anything but contempt.

He comes to rest on a spire. How could they have let it come this far? Beaten down and subservient, and still they remain quiet. They say, you do. *Creatures without direction endlessly seeking meaning.*

The scene around him flickers, a static burst and then nothing. He stands alone surrounded by darkness. A blue light flickers across the field of his vision, illuminating the figures in the dark. He hears voices, a language unknown to him. Niente smiles. 'Trust me to have a bad trip.'

He closes his eyes but the image remains the same, the flashing blue light, the smoke like darkness. His eyes open. The scene changes.

This vision is not his. A childhood nightmare that belongs to someone else. Niente's naked feet walk through the house, its lights dull, naked bulbs hanging like orange orbs struggling to cast glimmers of hope. He walks into the living room, two figures sit watching television through glazed eyes. His mother and father transfixed by the flickering static. Niente tries to call out to them, shouting but no words leave his throat. The only sound that of white noise. He screams but the constant hiss engulfs the sound, devouring it hungrily.

Then it comes, the sound he has been expecting. The pulsing hum, ebbing and flowing against the static, rising in volume. A twisted sound, dirty, throbbing. The heartbeat of the shadows. Soon it is the only sound he can hear, forcing itself upon him. Oppressive.

He turns and runs from the room, as he does he notices the delicate streams of blood trickling out of his parent's nostrils. He runs, he stops. The scene has changed again.

The pulse still fills his ears, but now its volume has decreased, echoing around the infinite space around him. Brightly lit and fluorescent harsh, his eyes try to adjust. At the centre of the space rises a pyramid of steps, all leading up to a chair. A solitary chair. Plain, wooden back and arms, metal legs. He frowns. An empty chair on a pyramid in nothing.

Niente lets his legs guide him up the steps. Each footstep bringing him closer to the chair. From the corners of his eyes he can see the darkness advancing with him. The once eternal light now a sea of inky black. He turns back to look the way he has come, staring into the heart of the darkness. He has done this; he brought the darkness into the dream of another. He steps backwards, his leg brushes against the chair. He turns, stumbling as he does so. He falls. Falls into the lap of a figure. His eyes rise slowly to the face. To his face.

He crawls backwards, taking in the image. Himself chained to the chair. The pulse of the dark increases. Louder and louder. He hears himself scream as the darkness engulfs everything.

*Present.*

One bursts into the office, the air cold from the wind whipping through the shattered window. He is surprised that no one had arrived yet, but guesses that it could have been any window; they all look the same from ground level. He also knows that Niente was not meant to be here. He should be at the rally. He is going to be late for his first big speech.

One looks, he sees Niente lying on the soft sofa facing the window. He rushes over; at least Niente had the sense to remove the needle. One's fingers grab at Niente's face, flicking open the eyelids with his thumbs. Glazed orbs of crystal blue look into nothing, bloodshot and vacant. *Why the fuck did you have to do this today?*

Niente mumbles, twists against One's grip. One moves his hand and grips Niente's shoulder, lifting him into a sitting position.

'Fuck off,' Niente groans distantly, raising his middle finger.

One smiles, at least he's kept his sense of humour. He slaps gently against Niente's cheeks. Niente groans in annoyance. One continues.

'Fuck off.' Niente's voice clearer. Angrier.

'You'll hate me for this,' One says. 'But fuck, you deserve it.' He pulls back his hand and slaps Niente as hard as he can. He lets go and jumps backwards.

Niente jumps unsteadily to his feet. 'You fucking wanker,' he shouts. 'I'm gonna fucking kill you.' He lunges at One who simply side steps and lets him crumple to the floor.

'What the hell are you playing at Niente?'

'One last trip, that's all it was.'

'Today? Couldn't you have waited? I should have predicted this.'

Niente sways as he sits. 'Call it courage.'

'I call it stupidity. We're gonna be late.'

'Always panicking about time, always rushing. We can't be late, they're all there for us.'

One snorts a chuckle. 'Always have an answer don't you.' He kicks Niente playfully.

Niente smiles. 'Yup,' he says like an excited five-year old.

'Right, let's get you sorted. Clean you up a bit.'

'Why? I'm alright, they'll all love me.'

'What? Doped up and clammy? No, you need a shower and a change of clothes. You can't do it dressed in those grotty things.'

Niente falls backwards, grumbling incoherently.

'No point resisting.' One grips Niente's skinny arms and drags him to his feet. Niente leans on him. One shakes his head with a smile. 'A cold shower and then it's your big day.'

He feels Niente begin to cry.

The stadium is a buzz of activity as their car pulls up to the gates. Niente looks away from the first suit he has ever worn and gazes out through the window, trying to take it all in. All those people here just for him. He lets his eyes pan across the building. Extravagant. *What am I doing?*

Their car pulls through the gates and parks in a designated place. Despite everything, they had actually arrived on time, well, give or take five minutes. His door is opened and he exits from the car. He can feel his heart pounding; nothing could have prepared him for this reality. He looks at One as he makes his way around the car to his side.

'You ready?' One asks.

'Not really.' Niente smiles.

'Your moment. This is for you alone.'

Niente hugs One, squeezing him tight. 'We all have to do what we have to do,' he whispers into One's ear. 'That's the way it's always been.'

One nods and as they pull apart Niente notices the tears in One's eyes.

'I guess this is it.' Niente smiles and turns to his bodyguards, who wait patiently for his instruction. 'Right, let's do this.'

Without looking back, Niente walks into the stadium leaving One standing alone by the car.

Niente follows his guards in silence as they lead him down the complex maze of corridors and stairs. He ignores everyone they pass, focusing on what he has to say. His visions made it clear. His piece has been played. Words formed and now everything is so pathetically unchangeable. He had made his secret choice and everyone has gathered in the hope of a new dawn, those who could not make it perched in anticipation in front of television screens. *Lost souls need a shepherd to follow.* He will give them what they wanted. He would be the first ray of the mourning sun.

His feet come to a stop. In front of him the solid doors stand closed. He looks at his guards and smiles. 'Let's get the show on the road.'

They nod and push open the doors. Niente steps out into the light.

The noise is deafening. Seventy thousand people cheering just for him. Applause and rapture his soundtrack as he walks from the doorway to the podium. From there he looks out into the crowds. Smiling faces and excited eyes. Across the city, a million minds focused on one twenty-nine year old. Niente, still young but with the weight of the world on his shoulders. In this moment, for once, he is truly lost for words.

Soon the cheering dies. Silence filling the space. Niente just stands watching. Everyone watches back, their arms by their sides. Everyone standing the same as their neighbours. He smiles coldly. Everybody hanging on his word, they would march to the beat of his drum if he told them to. How he wants to shake each one; it is time to masturbate to stimulate all those feelings they have been forced to numb.

Niente takes the final step closer to the microphones growing from the podium. He feels like a preacher about to teach the converted. The time has come. He opens his mouth and begins to speak.

'Who am I? I am an oncoming storm, an angel trapped in Hell. I burst into your lives, changed your outlook, helped you, supported you. I've made an unforgettable impact and then I'll be gone. Gone not by choice, just generally discarded. A thousand voices in my head talk to me. A life searching for happiness, searching for its goal.' He pauses, letting his projected voice echo back into the blissful silence.

'My piece has been played and time is running out. I could be a messiah and save you all from your fears. I want to reach into the heavens; I've done my practice and changed the lives of individuals, now let me change the lives of the many. Let me burn this world with revolution; let me bring about the end days.

'Who am I? Sometimes I don't know myself. I'm the ring on someone's finger, a name on your lips, a voice in a memory. I am a ghost. Give me your pain, your fears, your anger and I will give you love, give you compassion, give you direction. Heed my words or spend your days in regret.

'I am a living dream. The king, the final piece, the outcome creator. Waiting patiently. Moved one square at a time only when necessary. You fight your battles in front of me, marching your way to the end game. I'm a voice of reason in the dark.

'My eyes have seen the Other-side. The screaming, the pain. The darkness extending its tendrils; growing slowly from the corners. Its power reaching into your souls. The seeds of emptiness germinating, spreading their roots deep inside of you. As your hollowness grows count down the days. Once all your dreams and hopes have been engulfed only the darkness will remain. Empty souls lost and alone in fear.

'Who am I? I could be your saviour but no one is listening. I could be an angel. The antichrist. The king or the beast. But know that I am redemption; revenge will be my way. From the ebony snow did I rise; a devil's mark tattooed upon my flesh. We're entering into the end days. Pray death when your time comes.

'Who am I? I am an oncoming storm and still you welcome me with open arms. Don't you think that's a bit surreal?

'You may pray for forgiveness but your dreams plead for redemption. As this world turns in silence, just remember that I did this all for you.'

Niente steps back from the microphones. The silence remains until the last echo of his voice dies. Then the crowd cheers. Oh how they cheer, thick yells and whoops of pleasure. Sweeping and flowing like waves across the ocean, the noise breaking at his feet. They do not know why they are cheering; it had spread like wildfire, everyone following their neighbour. One cheer had started all this. One voice and like cattle they all followed. It feels so nice to be part of something.

And there in the center of the crowd, the ghost of young Tommy boy, fresh from suicide, the bullet wound pouring gored redemption down his back. He stands, watching in silence, praying his dreams will come.

Niente lets the cheering continue. His eyes pan the crowd. Brown folders with no flames. The red, the blue. The pawns intermingled with the set pieces. Everyone existing together in a shared harmony. Through the many faces, Niente's eyes lock onto One's. The scene slows. The cheers fade into the background and a moment is shared in that one motion. Two brothers look across the void of existence and deep into each other's soul. *Be warned creatures of deceit. Be warned of two brothers born of flesh and blood.*

Niente sees One smile. A cold, empty smile. He returns it, his last smile. This is redemption. Sacrifice the messiah to cleanse the soul. The bullet rips through his skull, his body slumps to the floor, the crowds fall silent. Cain kills Abel. The switch is flicked.

From behind his assassin the shadow rises. Tall, gaunt. Winged death swarming into the air. The crowds look to the heavens and see it, standing there framed by the clouds, eclipsing the sun, darkening the sky. Their jaws slacken and the shadow spreads its wings wide. Revealing the truth of humanity. A silent prayer of forgiveness crosses the land.

The light fades, the cloud of greed, hatred, pain and destruction blocks out the sun's dying glare.

$$O \quad + \quad I \quad = \quad \Phi$$

Nothing split by Unity is Phi, the constant of creation.